BIG WIN

Brit Boys Sports Romance

J.H. CROIX

J.H. CROIX

To the countless women who have found their way through to the other side of darkness.

Sign up for my newsletter for information on new releases!
http://jhcroixauthor.com/subscribe/

Follow me!
jhcroix@jhcroix.com
https://amazon.com/author/jhcroix
https://www.bookbub.com/authors/j-h-croix
https://www.facebook.com/jhcroix
https://www.instagram.com/jhcroix/

Chapter One

ALEX

My breath came in steady gusts as I ran along the walkway. It was barely past dawn, my favorite time of day, and I was out for my morning run. The park was quiet as I followed the path along the shore. Gulls called in the distance, the only noise to speak of at this hour. I ran for a solid half hour and slowed to a walk as I made my way through the forested part of the park back to my flat. The air was cool and damp, typical for a spring morning in Seattle. A sudden burst of chatter from squirrels in the trees caught my attention, and I glanced up to see a woman walking toward me with a giant dog at her side. Tall and stately, the dog walked with grace at her side. I didn't realize I'd stopped where I was until the woman got close enough for me to realize I knew her. A prickle of awareness ran up my spine.

Harper Jacobs was a good friend of my best mate's fiancée. Harper also got to me—big time. I couldn't put my finger on why. She was attractive, but in an understated way. I'd met her a bit ago when Liam, the best mate in question, invited me to meet him for coffee. Harper was there with Liam's fiancée Olivia. I'd encountered Harper a few more times since then, what with our respective friends head over heels in love. She was polite and friendly and always seemed to have an invisible bubble around her. I wanted to know why she kept herself protected like that. I waited for her to reach me, which she eventually did. She slowed to a stop, rested her hands on her hips and glanced up at me.

"Alex, right?" she asked.

"That would be me. I see you're out for a walk," I said, instantly wondering why I couldn't have slightly better conversational skills. Stating the obvious wasn't particularly inviting. I usually didn't give a bloody damn about conversing, but I wanted to know Harper beyond the superficial.

Harper nodded, her deep blue eyes crinkling at the corners with her small smile. "I am. I'm going to guess you're just finishing a run," she replied with a nod to my feet, which were encased in running shoes.

"That I am. I come here almost every day. I think I'd have seen you before if you're here often, what with...?" My words trailed off as I gestured to her giant dog.

"Stanley," she filled in, her smile stretching.

Damn. I wished I could see her smile more. Her whole face lit up and that careful, controlled look in her eyes softened.

As if in response to his name, Stanley stretched his head to my hand and slowly sniffed it. After a moment, he dipped his head further, nudging it under my hand as if he expected me to pet him. So I did. He was easily taller than my waist, his large eyes blue and his fur dappled steel gray.

"He likes you," Harper said. "Stanley can be picky, so take that as a compliment."

I stroked his head slowly and looked over at Harper. Her glossy brown hair was pulled back in a ponytail high atop her head with loose locks escaping. She blew a breath, effectively blowing one lock of hair out of her eyes. She wore fitted leggings and a fitted top, both bright blue, which brought out her eyes. She was clearly in good shape, but also managed to be curvy at the same time with full hips and generous breasts. I realized I was staring at her and forced myself to recall what she'd just said.

"I'll take it as a compliment then. What kind of dog is he?"

"Great Dane. He's on the large side for the breed, but he's nothing but a gentle giant." Her eyes canted down, and she laughed softly. Stanley had taken another step closer to me and nuzzled his massive head against my hip. "He's a lover, not a fighter," she said, looking back up to me. "So you run here on top of your practices?" she asked, referencing my career as a goalkeeper for the Seattle Stars.

I was a Seattle transplant after moving here with three of my teammates from our former team in London. The Seattle Stars were America's current best hope for a shot at international glory on the soccer stage. Though I still felt out of step with Seattle and America in general, none of it helped by the fact they insisted on calling football soccer here, I'd come to enjoy Seattle and the team. Being a professional footballer, or professional sports player of any kind really, meant you went where you had the best offer. Oh, there were negotiations and such, but that was the life. Well that, and dedicating your mind and body to a sport. I loved football and had loved it since I was a lad. I felt lucky to be able to play professionally.

I met Harper's clear blue gaze and nodded. "Most days I run on my own before practice."

She nodded, but was otherwise quiet. The silence started to stretch, but it was a comfortable silence. In the few times I'd been around Harper, we'd always been in a group, usually with our shared friends. It occurred to me just now I didn't know much about her, other than who her friends were. Stanley nudged my hand, and I realized I'd slacked in petting him. "Sorry 'bout that, Stanley," I said, glancing down and stroking his sleek head again.

"I suppose you need to go," Harper said.

When I looked back at her, she looked, well the only way to describe it was nervous. Seeing as I hadn't a clue what she could be nervous about, I was flummoxed. But I didn't want her to go. I wanted to curl my hand around hers and walk through the park.

"Why don't we walk for a bit?" I asked, startling myself.

Her eyes widened for a beat, and her cheeks flushed. She went still, so still it worried me, and that controlled look slipped in front of her eyes again. Stanley took a step away from me and nudged her hip gently before turning to stand close beside her. He exuded a quiet protectiveness toward her. Her shoulders rose and fell with a deep breath, and then she nodded. "Okay, that would be nice."

I bit back my grin and turned to walk alongside her. Stanley padded beside us. He wasn't on a leash and didn't appear to need one. He stayed right by Harper's side and walked quietly, his gaze alert. Aside from the squirrels and birds chattering around us, it felt as if we were alone. Oh, there were a few other early risers out and about, but anyone here at this hour loved the quiet as much as I did. Harper idly kicked a pebble as we walked. I wanted to look long and hard in her eyes and make the underlying worry and tension in them disappear. Yet, I was slightly relieved we weren't face to face because Harper seemed more relaxed when I wasn't looking right at her.

So I just kept walking. I didn't care to talk. Talking wasn't really my thing. As we walked along, I felt the hum of tension emanating from Harper start to ease. Lincoln Park was an urban sanctuary and preserve situated by Puget Sound. There were the usual park amenities, such as a pool and tennis courts, but there was also a walkway along the beautiful shoreline and a well-preserved old growth forest, offering plenty of peaceful walking in the quiet hours of the day. We followed a footpath through the trees until we reached the walkway where I'd gone for my run this morning.

Salty air gusted off Puget Sound with the sun rising through the clouds. I glanced to the side when Stanley stopped abruptly. Stanley was staring straight ahead at a man running along the walkway. He didn't raise his hackles, nor did he make a sound, but it was plain he was bothered. I lifted my eyes to Harper. Splotchy red spread up her neck and face, and she looked absolutely horrified. She seemed to have forgotten I was there. I reached for her hand, curled tight in a fist at her side. The second I touched her, she swatted my hand away and then gasped.

"Oh, I'm sorry! I, um, I..." She looked from me back to the man, whoever the hell he was, running toward us. He was still a good distance away. I didn't know what was going on, but I had two inclinations—go punch the guy because his mere existence upset Harper, or get Harper away from him.

Liam was wont to tease me for 'protecting the whole wide world' as he liked to put it. I didn't like seeing anyone hurt. Ever. I had my reasons, but those weren't particularly important now. What mattered was taking care of Harper.

"Harper?"

I wanted to reach for her hand again, but I didn't want to startle her as I already had. Her eyes flicked to me again. The blue had gone darker, but she held still. "I'm not sure what's up, but I think we should go," I finally said.

She nodded jerkily, but she didn't move. So I reached for her hand, and this time she let me curl mine over hers. I don't know how long she'd been cold, but right now, her hand was freezing. Stanley was still staring at the man gradually closing the distance between us. I'd seen him running before and thought nothing of it. Whatever he was to Harper, it wasn't good. "Stanley, come on," I said softly as I turned and led Harper away.

The next few minutes were quiet. I didn't even notice the birds calling and the squirrels chattering as we made our way back through the trees to the park entrance. I'd walked here, but I didn't know how Harper had arrived, nor did I know where she lived, but I wasn't leaving her side until she was home again. We reached the park entrance, and I glanced down. Her skin was pale and her eyes shuttered. Stanley was as close as he could get to her on the other side without melding his body to hers.

After a moment, Harper looked up. "Did you walk here or drive?" I asked.

"I walked," she said, her voice low and quiet.

"Okay, where to?"

She looked confused. "I'm walking you home," I explained.

She started to shake her head, but I shook mine in return. "This isn't up for debate. You don't have to tell me what's got you so upset, but there's no bloody way I'm leaving you here with that look on your face. I'll walk you right to your door and you can slam it in my face, but I'm not letting you walk alone."

She swallowed and then nodded. "I live just a few blocks that way," she said pointing the same direction I'd walk to return to my flat. This area of Seattle was residential with a mix of homes and flats.

"Perfect. You must live a few blocks from me then. Shall we?"

At her small nod, I commenced to walk

again, her hand still in mine. Her hand was finally starting to absorb heat from mine, which relieved me. I kept batting away thoughts about what may have put the stark fear in her gaze, but I didn't want to think about that now. I just wanted to make sure she got home.

I realized I hadn't been paying much attention to how fast I was walking. I tended to move quickly no matter the circumstance. I glanced to Harper, about to slow down, but she was keeping pace easily even if she still looked half-stunned. We crossed another street, and Harper slowed. My flat was another two blocks away. "It's here," she said, pointing up to an older home, clearly renovated into smaller flats. Flowers were blooming in abundance in boxes hung on windowsills and railings.

"I'll walk you in."

Her eyes gave little away, but she looked the tiniest bit relieved and nodded. After she keyed in a combination at the main entrance, which led into a massive foyer, we made our way up two flights of stairs that hugged the curved wall. I released her hand on the way up and stood beside her while she pulled her keys out of her jacket. They fell to the floor in a clatter. It appeared that each floor held a single flat with Harper's door the only one up here on the top floor.

"Dammit," she said in a whisper, promptly dropping them again when she tried to fit the key in the lock.

"Let me," I said, reaching down and scooping up the keys.

She was quiet while I slid the key into the lock. I felt entirely out of place and as if I was probably pushing into places I shouldn't go, but I didn't feel right leaving just now. Despite the fact I didn't know Harper particularly well, she was important to Olivia who had essentially become the center of my best mate's universe. By extension of that, she mattered to me, even setting aside the draw I felt for her. I needed to make sure she was okay before I left her, and she'd been anything but since she'd laid eyes on that man in the park.

When the door opened, I held it and gestured Harper through, stepping just beyond the threshold myself. Stanley stood beside Harper, his eyes on her as if he was trying to ascertain her status. She stopped after several steps and hugged her arms around her waist, a visible shiver running through her. That was it. I was making tea.

"How about I make you some tea?" I asked.

Her eyes swung to mine, almost incredulous. "Tea?"

"Yes, tea. You're shivering, and I don't know what happened back there or who that man was, but it upset you. Us Brits happen to think tea makes everything better. At the least, it should warm you up a bit."

She stared at me for a beat and then smiled, just the smallest smile. "Okay. That would be nice." For the first time since we'd seen that man, she seemed to relax a bit.

Her flat was on the small side. We'd entered into what must be the living room, which had a window taking up the entire side facing the street and offered a view of Puget Sound in the distance. Light fell in a shaft from the sun rising up above the water. The hardwood floor gleamed under the sun. A cream colored circular rug sat in the center of the room with a sectional couch surrounding it. A TV was mounted on the wall above a small fireplace. The kitchen was to the side with an island demarcating the space from the living room. A door leading to a bathroom and another to what I presumed to be her bedroom were at the back.

She gestured to the kitchen. "By all means, make some tea."

It wasn't hard to figure out what was where, what with a tea kettle on her stove. With that and water, all we had to do was wait. It occurred to me I hadn't asked about the most important part. "I'm assuming you actually have some tea," I said, glancing to Harper who'd followed me around the island and was presently leaning against the counter. The lines of tension had eased on her face, and she finally looked back to herself. She grinned. "I do. Right over there," she said, pointing to a cabinet behind me.

I started to open it and then paused. "Is it okay if...?"

"Of course it's okay. If it wasn't okay, I'd have shooed you out already," she said with another grin.

I liked Harper grinning, liked it quite a lot.

Chapter Two

HARPER

Alex Gordon was standing in the kitchen in my new apartment making me tea. The incongruity of it made me almost laugh aloud, but I bit it back because he was being so sweet about the whole thing. He turned back to the cabinet and started rummaging through the tea boxes in there, eventually pulling out a box of, you guessed it, English breakfast tea. It was morning, and he was British. It made such perfect sense, I finally started laughing when he turned around with the box in hand.

Alex arched a brow, a smile playing at the corners of his mouth. "Something funny?" he asked, appearing slightly confused at my laughter.

If he was confused, well so was I, but I wasn't in the mood to ponder it. I had no sense of how much time had passed since I'd seen the man from my nightmares jogging our way in the park this morning, but thanks to Alex, I'd managed to swat those feelings away. The relief was so great, I was off kilter. Well, that and the fact that Alex was here.

Alex was so handsome, it bordered on ridiculous. He had brown hair that verged on curly and was often rumpled as it was now. Gorgeous chocolate brown eyes were paired with that hair. Beyond the fact he had a body that was all muscle and nothing else, the chiseled features of his face with classic cheekbones and a straight blade of a nose combined together to make him pure eye candy. To make matters worse, he appeared oblivious to his devastating effect on women and tended to be aloof and quiet.

I'd met Alex in passing through Olivia and her fiancée Liam. Olivia was one of my closest friends and had fallen hard for Liam Reed who happened to sign with the Seattle Stars along with Alex and two other British soccer players. Alex was famous for his unshakable nerves under pressure as the goalkeeper, and thus far this season, he'd yet to allow a single goal from an opposing team into the net. I'd previously paid little attention to the international fervor over soccer, but Olivia had begun bringing me to games with her occasionally, so I had an idea of how compelling Alex was.

I hadn't let myself think much about how swoon-worthy he was, but right here, right now with him in my kitchen, it was hard to ignore—soccer star and sex symbol wrapped up in a body so yummy, he made me want to lick him all over. His presence up close was intense, yet comforting at once. He exuded a quiet power. Just now, I started to laugh again when I realized he was patiently waiting for me to answer. I pointed to the mugs I'd set on the counter, and he shook his head slightly as he stepped past me to drop tea bags in them. He turned and leaned into the corner of the counter, just a foot or so away from me.

I sobered when it occurred to me I must seem half crazy to him. He happened to have been with me at an incredibly inopportune time there in the park. I didn't want him to think I needed protecting, although I was incredibly relieved he had been there and had guided me out of the park. With Stanley on one side and Alex on the other, I'd numbly made my way home. Alex's kind gesture of making tea snapped me out of where I'd gone inside. It was so funny to see this big, strong, powerful man offer to make tea.

I caught his eyes and flutters twirled in my belly. I managed to take a breath. I felt strange—hyperaware and restless. The awful truth behind why I'd gotten so scared this morning made me want to prove it had no effect on me anymore. We stared at each other, Alex's gaze coasting over me. He wasn't particularly easy to read, but I sensed an answering desire in him. My hands were curled on the edge of the counter, and I realized I was gripping it. I eased my grip and pushed away, my body humming and my mind driven to wipe out everything threatening to take over.

I stepped right in front of Alex, the heat of his body emanating. Getting close to him was like being beside a livewire—energy and power vibrated from him. His breath hissed when I stepped even closer. There was a part of me that thought I was completely out of my mind and perhaps I was. But dammit, I wasn't going to keep letting my life be ruled by one ugly incident. Alex stood before me and the air around us was taut under the force shimmering between us. I could either let myself stumble backwards, or let this moment envelop me instead.

With my pulse thundering in my ears and heat shooting through me, I slid a hand up Alex's arm. Oh wow. Just touching his arm was all kinds of amazing. He didn't move as I stroked over his muscles, savoring the feel of their strength and subtle power. His skin was warm to the touch and sleek. I didn't stop and coasted up over his t-shirt to curl around his neck. Thought fled, and I moved on instinct. His mouth was delectable with generous lips and a dimple just under his bottom lip. I curled my hand around his neck and pulled him toward me.

He stopped, maybe an inch away from me. "Harper?"

"Hm?"

"What are you doing?"

"Kissing you," I replied.

His chocolate brown gaze locked with mine, searching. I didn't know what he saw there, but I could see the beat of his pulse in his neck, and his breath was shallow. Impatient, I yanked him to me. The moment our mouths collided, it was as if I'd been shocked. A hot jolt scored through me. He froze, and then looped his arms around me, pulling me up against him. Oh, this was perfect. Being held against his hard, hot body was heaven. He slid a palm up my back and curled it around my neck. Our kiss went from a stunning point of contact to a deep dive into pure deliciousness. I'd have guessed Alex to be a patient man, which made him an incredible kisser. He didn't rush and he didn't go all caveman and stuff his tongue down my throat. Oh no. He was slow and devastating with soft kisses, sweeps of his tongue against mine and nibbles on my bottom lip. All of it leading up to a kiss so melting, I truly would have collapsed had he not been holding me.

He drew back and tucked his head into the curve of my neck. I was relieved because I didn't know if I could bear to look at him just now. I'd meant to kiss him as some sort of bold move, as much for myself as anyone, to show I couldn't be cowed by the past. I hadn't known kissing Alex would be what that was—a heady, encompassing madness that made me feel more alive than I'd ever felt. Eventually he lifted his head and eased his hold. I hadn't realized my feet had actually been off the ground until he slowly let me slide down his body. I could feel the ridge of his arousal against me, and my body's answering clench.

When my feet were on the ground again,

I took a deep breath and stepped back. His eyes were waiting for me when I looked up. "What was that about?" he asked.

Excellent question, and one that had layers of answers. Right now, I couldn't quite contemplate anything beyond this immediate moment. "I wanted to kiss you," I finally said. A perfectly true answer, but it didn't capture everything I felt, certainly not the way I felt now.

Chapter Three

ALEX

"Bloody hell," I mumbled to myself as I looked down the long hallway inside the stadium to see Liam standing with our Coach and two reporters just outside the media room.

We'd had our first loss of the season today. One goal—just one—was all that had gotten by me this season so far, but that's all it took for the other team to win. Truth was, they'd played a stellar game. I'd blocked a number of shots at the goal before one slipped by me and just barely. I squared my shoulders and made my way down the hallway. Coach Bernie had given me a ten minute reprieve after the game because he knew I bloody hated interviews. I sent a silent thanks to Liam. Not only was he my best mate and had been since we were boys, but he took the brunt of the publicity front for me. With me as goalkeeper and him as playmaker on the team, we were often called upon to play nice with the sports media. Liam wasn't any fonder of it than I was, but he was more jovial by nature. In short, he was better with bollocks.

I reached the group and went to stand by Liam. Coach gave me a subtle nod, his blue eyes warm. Last year, I'd been a bit relieved to get the offer from the Seattle Stars. Don't get me wrong, I loved playing ball no matter where I played, but I'd been caught in a power struggle on our last team back in London. A power struggle between the goalkeeper who'd come before me and the coach who'd relegated him to back-up goalkeeper after one too many times he'd shown up for practice still sloshed from a night of partying. I'd been happy to take on the starting role because I knew I was a stronger player, but I'd bloody hated the tension. When things went sideways for us at the end of the season and my agent dangled the offer from Seattle in front of me, I jumped at it. It helped to have Liam and two others mates from London along for the ride.

I hadn't known what to expect from our new Coach, but Bernie Hoffman didn't brook any drama. The nonsense that happened on my last team? A definite *no* on this team. Coach came to his role with years of experience as an international soccer star back in his day over fifteen years ago. He was well respected by players worldwide after being a dominant player in his era. He was rock-solid in confidence and work ethic, and expected the same from us. I met his nod with my own and swallowed my frustration. I felt like I'd let the whole team down.

As we followed the interviewers into the media room, Liam leaned toward me. "Mate, ease up. I can see you giving yourself bloody hell in that big brain of yours. Coach chewed out Ethan and two other defenders for leaving too many openings in front of the goal, so don't go thinking you're holding the bag alone."

I glanced to Liam whose bright blue eyes were twinkling. They were almost always twinkling. With his black hair and those eyes, he'd been fodder for the gossip pages back in Britain. I wanted nothing to do with publicity like that, so I ignored it completely. I met Liam's gaze and shook my head. "Still shouldna missed the stop." I didn't offer more, but thrashed myself mentally. I'd been a hair too slow and that's all it took for us to lose the game.

Liam clapped me on the shoulder. "This'll only make us stronger. It's never good to go into the playoffs without at least one loss behind us. Makes us too cocky."

I might have agreed on that point, but it didn't make me feel any better. We reached the table and slipped into the chairs flanking Coach. The next twenty minutes or so rolled by in a blur. I tried to keep from looking too grim, which Liam had jokingly noted I tended to do even when we won. I was relieved when we walked out of the room and down the hall. All I wanted now was to shower and go home to watch replays, so I could sort out if there was any way to make sure today's miss never happened again.

I ignored everyone as I stepped into the locker room. A short while later, I rubbed a towel over my hair and tossed it into the hamper nearby. A few teammates were still around, including Liam and Ethan Walsh. Like Liam and me, Ethan was a British boy. He'd gone to university with us. He'd initially signed with a different team back in Britain, but then joined us and signed on to the Stars when they dangled good offers in front of us. I closed my locker and went to sit down across from where they sat on a bench running the length of one wall of lockers.

"Well, guess it's best to lose now than later, eh?" I asked.

Ethan glanced over and shrugged. "Bollocks," he said with a wink. Ethan was as jovial by nature as Liam. If possible, he was even more of a flirt. Liam had been a perpetual tease when it came to women until he'd fallen head over heels in love with Olivia. With Ethan's shaggy golden hair and green eyes, he'd been dubbed the "Golden Boy Brit." He found no end of amusement in this. Despite his tendency to joke, I knew he was just as bothered as I was over our loss. He played the left wingback position and was one of our best defenders.

I met his wink with a shrug and leaned forward, resting my elbows on my knees as I looked to Liam. "Surprised to see you still here. Shouldn't you be off snogging your girl somewhere?"

Liam flashed a grin. "Right you are, mate. I should be. But I'm not. Olivia texted and said I'm supposed to bring you mates with me to dinner with her and her friends."

Ethan arched a brow. "Told him you'd try

to say no, so he made me wait so I could badger you into it," he said with a slight grin.

I glanced between them and bit back a sigh. I was tired and not exactly feeling social on the heels of our loss. "Tonight?"

Liam stood up. "Tonight. Something to do with Daisy winning a research award. Harper will be there too."

The moment he mentioned that, my answer was a definite yes. But I wasn't about to let on. No one knew I fancied Harper. Fancy wasn't quite up to speed. More like burning hot lust for the girl. It had been a full week since I'd encountered her in the park, and I'd thought about that kiss a few hundred times since then. Suddenly, a social burden became an opportunity. I might've wanted to say no, but Liam wasn't my best mate for nothing. If he wanted me somewhere, I was usually there. I stood. "Okay, mate. Anything for Olivia," I said with a roll of my eyes.

Ethan looked slightly surprised, but he stood and walked outside with us. We took a cab to a small Thai restaurant not far from where my flat was. My body was thrumming with anticipation at seeing Harper again. Even I had to admit to myself that my interest in her was out of my control. Before last week, I'd found her interesting and had been drawn to see behind the invisible walls she kept around herself. Between watching her withdraw into a place of fear after seeing that man in the park and rebounding back to boldly kiss me, well, it was safe to say I was bloody determined to crack through her façade. That and do a hell of a lot more than kiss her. Her kiss had been so bold, I got hard just thinking about it.

Downside to being a professional footballer was the flood of women draping themselves about my teammates and me made it hard to be interested. I was immune to the usual cloying charms of women chasing after nothing more than a notch on their bedpost. Harper was different, precisely because until she kissed me, she'd seemed beyond indifferent.

When we walked into the restaurant, my eyes found Harper immediately. She was walking toward the table where Olivia sat with their friend Daisy. Harper's hips swayed with each step. Her hair was pulled back in a ponytail, as it almost always was. She slipped into the booth, opposite Olivia and Daisy, and I extended my stride, determined to claim the seat beside her. Liam was so focused on Olivia—she was all he focused on in life aside from playing ball—he didn't notice my attention on Harper. Ethan, however, did.

"Well, well," he murmured slyly. "Look who has a thing for Harper."

I elbowed him in the side right before we reached the booth. "Stuff it."

I ignored Ethan's choked laugh and smoothly slipped into the booth beside Harper. Ethan, being the solid mate he was, promptly slid in on my other side, crowding me against Harper. He might enjoy teasing a bit too much, but he was solid in every way. If he thought I liked Harper, he'd throw his efforts into smoothing the way for me. At the moment, I glanced to him and chuckled.

Ethan winked and promptly turned to flirt with the waitress. "Hello luv, bring my boys some beers. We lost and we need to drown our sorrows." The waitress in question, an older woman with glossy black hair, dark eyes, and slim figure, grinned right back at him. "Coming right up."

Liam glanced to our side of the booth and down to Olivia. "Scootch over, luv. If the boys can fit over there, I can fit here."

Olivia, as besotted with Liam as he was with her, nudged Daisy in the shoulder. Liam sat down beside her and landed a kiss on her neck. Olivia, whom I'd liked the moment I met her, flushed. She glanced over to us. "Hi guys, sorry about the game."

"Eh. We took it on the chin," Ethan replied.

Olivia's dark hair was tied back in a knot, which bounced when she nodded. "Right then. No need to dwell." Her green gaze flicked to me. "Thanks for coming, Alex. I thought..."

Daisy cut in. "She thought you guys needed something to take your mind off the loss," she offered bluntly.

Ethan threw a grin at Daisy. I glanced between them and realized they matched. Each had blonde locks and happened to be wearing green shirts this evening. Daisy's brown eyes flicked to Ethan and away, a quick flash of curiosity I almost missed in her gaze. Ethan stared at her a few beats longer than usual, leading me to wonder what he was thinking. Rather than wondering for long, I glanced to Harper who was sitting quietly beside me.

I could feel the tension humming in her body and wanted to slide my arm around her shoulder and somehow ease it. If only I knew where it came from. Instead, I reminded myself where we were and ordered my body to behave. My cock twitched—because just being this close to Harper made blood shoot straight to it—but I managed. "Hello Harper," I said as I waited for her to look up.

She did, and those bright blue eyes of hers widened slightly when they landed on me. "Hey Alex," she said softly, her expression holding that careful control I'd only seen fall twice before—first in fear and then in desire. I didn't ever want to see fear on her face again, but desire... Oh yes, I wanted to see more of that. I didn't know how I knew it, but Harper had an intensity to her that made me know, just know, she'd be beyond wild if she ever let go.

Daisy said something, and Harper's gaze snapped away from mine as she replied. I'd wanted to see her, but bloody hell, this was inconvenient. I'd underestimated her effect on me. I'd seen her around enough, yet this was the first time I'd seen her since she kissed me senseless. Oh, I took control of the kiss once it started, but make no mistake, she started it. Her boldness, hidden behind her controlled façade, nearly set me on fire.

The waitress arrived and delivered our beer. Liam ordered drunken noodles for all of us, declaring we'd love them. Meanwhile, conversation carried on around me. This was nothing unusual for me. I enjoyed my mates, yet never felt much need to talk. What I wanted right now was to be alone with Harper. Since that wasn't an option, I'd take what I could have. With Daisy bantering with, well, everyone but Harper and me, I looked to Harper to find her blue gaze waiting.

My cock twitched again, and I ignored it. "Haven't see you at the park again," I said, promptly regretting my comment. I might not know why, but I'd wager Harper had no interest in setting foot in the park again if it meant she might encounter the man who'd made her freeze in fear from afar. I'd seen him again myself from a distance. Had we been alone, I might've considered approaching him. But the park had been busy with runners, walkers and the like, so I'd ignored him.

Harper shook her head, her glossy dark hair swinging to and fro in its ponytail. "I haven't been. I, um..." She paused and worried her bottom lip between her teeth. Bloody hell. She needed to stop that, or my cock would stand at attention again. As it was, it was at half-mast every moment I was near her.

When the moment of silence stretched, I felt inclined to reassure her. "You don't need to explain. I can guess at why you might not go to the park. If you *do* want to go, just tell me when and I'll meet you there."

I meant it, yet my words startled me. I wasn't one to rush or push. No, rather I held back. I liked women quite well. I just didn't like the publicity associated with trying to date whilst under the microscope of being a sports star. Back in London, I had some arrangements that suited me well. I could take care of my needs, leave women satisfied and keep it out of the press. It wasn't what you might think. I don't mean I paid women to have sex with me. Rather, I lucked into meeting a young widow who absolutely wasn't looking for love, but she had needs, same as me. My connection to her led me to another woman, this one no widow, but in a chaste marriage—a quite public marriage. Once again, a woman who had needs and required the same privacy I preferred.

Before you go thinking I thought it was okay to bust in on someone's marriage, it wasn't quite like that. They'd married because they were best friends and for business reasons. In some ways, it seemed from the outside they had a better marriage than many people I knew. They respected each other and cared about each other. They just didn't consider sex part of their marriage. Not a choice I'd be inclined to make, but not my place to judge. Since moving to Seattle, I was in a bit of a dry spell. A visit or two to London wasn't quite meeting my needs. So perhaps, my cock had a few opinions on the matter.

Nothing with Harper was about simple physical need. Meanwhile, in the vein of pure physical need, Harper was like a jolt of adrenaline to my sex drive—she by herself was the magic ingredient. Did I say bloody hell yet? Because, dammit, I needed to get a handle on myself.

Before I could think to correct my offer, Harper's eyes searched my face. After a moment, one corner of her mouth kicked up. "You'd run with me?" she asked.

Just that, barely a smile from Harper, and it felt like the sun coming out. Aside from the simple fact I enjoyed her smile, she had a delectable mouth. Her face was usually held tight, but when she relaxed, even a little, her mouth did too. Her lips were plump and full. I knew precisely how they felt under mine— soft, lush and mobile. She angled her head to the side in question, and it suddenly occurred to me I hadn't answered her.

"I would," I said.

"Oh," she said, the single word coming

out on a breath. I could see her pulse beating at her throat and wanted to lick it. Not now though. Not with the hum of conversation around us and the curious eyes that would surely turn our way if I acted on my impulse.

"Do you run every day?" she asked.

"Most days."

"What time?"

"Eh, usually six or so."

Her eyes were thoughtful and turned inward again. I could feel her thinking. "I like to run and so does Stanley," she said suddenly. "If you tell me when, I'll meet you there."

I felt as if she'd handed me a present. I slipped my hand in my jeans pocket and pulled out my phone. "Here, put your number in. Password's Queen34." I said, handing it to her.

"You want me to just put my number in your phone? And you're telling me your password? Are you out of your mind?" she asked, her surprise wiping that controlled expression off of her face.

I shrugged. "Don't think so. I've got nothing to hide. Put your number in and I'll text you in the mornings before I go. I run right by your building, so we can start there."

"Trust me, Harper, Alex has nothing to hide. No naughty pics for you to find on his phone. Probably not even any juicy phone numbers," Liam said with a grin.

Harper looked from me to him and started laughing. Daisy cocked a brow. "Wow, you've got moves, Alex."

I glanced her way quizzically.

"Making Harper laugh takes special skills." Daisy's eyes flicked to Harper who was tapping in my password. "Is it that silly password that's got you laughing? Why Queen34?" Daisy asked, her eyes swinging back to me.

"Because I like Queen," I explained.

"The band?" Daisy asked next.

At my nod, Daisy grinned. "They're one of Harper's old faves, right Harper?"

Harper's eyes bounced from my phone to Daisy to me, a slow grin stretching across her face. Damn. She could smile forever. I loved it that much. Only downside: my cock kept twitching. Harper's smile, her real smile, not the polite one I'd seen before, transformed her face—her eyes held a wicked glint, her lush mouth softened, and a dimple appeared in one cheek. "True. Hard to find any band to compare to Queen, especially these days," she replied before glancing back to my phone as she keyed her number in my contacts.

Harper handed my phone back to me

right when Daisy said something else, but I didn't hear her. If Daisy had been talking to me, she moved on, asking Ethan something about something. Harper caught my eyes. "I'm up early no matter what, but I don't want you to think I expect you to meet me every day," she said, a subtle flush cresting her cheekbones.

Oh, she'd be seeing me every bloody day now. Truthfully, I did run most days, so it wasn't out of my way. I wasn't ready to tell her I was bound and determined to see her every chance I could get now that I'd had a taste of her. Nor was I about to tell her I was determined to find out what lay behind her controlled façade. But I would tell her the simple truth. "Like I said, I'm there practically every day as it is. You'll see me. Expect a text tomorrow morning."

She nodded quickly and looked away, responding to something Olivia said. A bit later after we'd had our fill of drunken noodles and drinks, the impromptu gathering broke apart. Liam strolled out at Olivia's side, his hand tucked in the back pocket of her jeans. The man was beyond besotted with her and didn't even care to hide it. Daisy and Ethan had left a few minutes prior with Harper right behind them. I'd beaten back the urge to follow her.

I returned to the booth to toss a tip on the table after a trip to the rest room and made my way outside. It had started to rain. There were many things I liked about Seattle, and while I couldn't say I liked the rain per se, I didn't mind it most of the time.

Tonight, I'd forgotten my jacket, so it was a slight inconvenience. Blocks from my flat, I wasn't about to bother with a cab. I put my head down and walked through the rain. By the time I reached my building, my shirt was soaked through, but I felt refreshed. I stopped at the base of the stairs to my building and glanced underneath. A pair of eyes glittered in the light cast from the streetlights. "Hey Callie," I said in greeting to the small cat who'd taken up residence under the stairs. I'd named her Callie because she was a calico and because I hadn't thought she'd really stick around. Yet, she had. She'd been appearing under the front steps for two months now. My goal was to get her inside with my landlord's permission already granted. But Callie was on the shy side. It had taken over a month to get her to the point where she didn't bolt when I greeted her. I reached a hand under the steps and held it still. She carefully sniffed at it, but declined to move. It was damp under there, but she was out of the worst of the rain.

"What's under there?"

The voice sent a prickle down my spine. I straightened to find Harper walking up behind me. Her flat was another two blocks past mine, so it made perfect sense she'd be returning home the same way. Yet, in all the time I'd lived here, I'd never seen her around. She had her hood pulled up over her head, the water running in rivulets down the sides and dripping on her cheeks.

I took a breath and eyed her. "A cat. She showed up a while ago. I'm hoping she'll come inside soon, but she's pretty skittish."

Harper stared at me for a few beats before a slow smile spread across her face. Her smile was becoming a problem. I wanted to tug her to me and lay another kiss on those delicious lips.

HARPER

I looked up at Alex and fought to keep from laughing. This man, tall and so fit every inch of him appeared sculpted from stone, was trying to sweet talk a cat. I hadn't been able to stop thinking about our kiss—the recollection was seared into my body and brain. Yet, I'd somehow convinced myself in the intervening week that I'd imagined the chemistry between us. I'd been definitively wrong. The second I saw him, I was reminded he was like flint to stone. He struck sparks inside me that threatened to send me up in flames.

He stood before me, his presence strong and quiet. His shirt was wet and outlined every inch of his muscled chest and arms. He was all corded muscle and sinew. Once again,

I wanted to lick him all over—he looked so deliciously sexy. I was used to being around athletes and generally found myself unmoved by them. As a physical therapist, my days were a mix of working with patients who were recovering from various injuries. When it came to the male athletes, they were so often arrogant, it was annoying. Alex was a different beast altogether. Despite his stature as a professional soccer player, internationally renowned before he ever landed in Seattle after helping his team in England win a World Cup, Alex was low-key. He conveyed an intense level of confidence, but not an ounce of arrogance.

I realized I was doing nothing other than standing there staring at him in the rain. With a mental shake, I dragged my thoughts off of their lascivious turn. "A cat, huh? How do you know she's a she?" I managed to ask.

He cocked his head to the side, his mouth curling up at one corner. *Oh. My.* My pulse went from fast to racing and my low belly clenched. I'd thought myself permanently over anything resembling lust. Yet, all Alex had to do was grin and it felt as if fireworks had been set off inside of me.

"I don't know actually. She just seems like

a she. She's never let me close enough to check."

I leaned down and peered under the stairs to see a small, bedraggled cat nestled into a blanket under the bottom step. 'She' was wet, but seemed comfortable enough. I straightened and looked back up at Alex. "Did you put that blanket under there?"

He lifted a shoulder in a shrug. "Maybe."

A small laugh sputtered out before I could stop it. "We'd better not let it get out that the Stars goalie is such a softie he put a blanket out for a cold kitty."

Unbothered, Alex simply shrugged again. "Feel free to make fun."

"Have you tried luring her out with food?"

He nodded, his brown eyes twinkling. "Sure did. She ate the food, but wasn't coming out. She used to run off anytime I got close and now she doesn't, so I'm figuring eventually she'll come inside."

I nodded just as a small gust of wind blew my hood back and sent drizzle pelting against my cheeks. A car rolled to a stop at the stoplight, and I reflexively glanced over, my gut coiling with dread the moment I saw the driver's profile. In the shadowed light from the streetlights, the man's face was illuminated.

I'd recognize Joe Schmidt anywhere. This was now the second time I'd seen him in the neighborhood. I wished I'd known he lived nearby before I signed the lease on my new apartment. For the first time since he raped me four years ago, I hadn't tried to find out where he was. I didn't like thinking about Joe and had finally believed I'd made progress when I moved to a new place. I forced my gaze away and tried to beat back the icy cold anxiety knotting in my chest.

I pulled my hood back up and focused on breathing to try to stay calm. Alex's voice broke into my awareness. I glanced up to see his eyes flick from the car at the stoplight where Joe still sat in his car and back to me. If he happened to notice anything, he didn't let on. "How about some tea?" he asked suddenly.

"Tea? Now?"

"Sure. It's cold and rainy. I'll walk you home after."

I couldn't bear to tell him I didn't want to walk home alone all of the sudden. As out of the blue his invitation for tea seemed, I grabbed onto it. "Tea would be great," I said, forcing some cheer into my tone.

Alex slid his arm over my shoulders, as if it was the most natural thing in the world to do, and guided me up the steps. Moments later, I followed him into his apartment. I knew he'd once shared this place with Liam, but I'd never been here. Until I'd encountered him at the park last week, I didn't know he lived anywhere near where I'd moved. We entered into an actual entryway with closets on either side and a tiled floor, convenient given my jacket was dripping wet. Without a word, Alex hung my jacket on a coatrack by the door once I peeled it off. I followed his lead and kicked my shoes off before stepping into the living room. In the living room, a large sectional couch faced a television mounted on the wall with a cushioned ottoman in between. Beyond this area was a kitchen against the back wall with a half wall serving as a divider.

The living room had wall-to-wall carpeting of soft gray, while his couch was charcoal gray. The only dash of color in the room was a bright blue blanket thrown on the back of the couch. Alex glanced my way as he headed toward what appeared to be the bathroom. There were three doors leading off the living room. I ascertained the other two were bedrooms. Before I realized what he was doing, he'd peeled his wet shirt off and tossed it in a hamper just inside the bathroom door.

Given his shirt was wet, this was the logical thing to do. Nothing wrong with a guy changing his shirt. Knowing Alex's life as a professional athlete, I knew he was likely oblivious to changing in front of anyone, seeing as he did it day in and day out in the locker room.

When he turned through the door into what must be his bedroom, my mouth went dry. Okay. It's not like I didn't know he was handsome and built. I'd gotten a sense of how amazing his body was when I kissed him. The failure of my imagination was revealed just now. Oh. My. God. He was beyond perfect. I could actually count his abs. There were, in fact, six clearly visible. His soccer player's build wasn't mere bulk, rather it was toned perfection, every muscle outlined for me to see. Even his back was a work of art, his shoulders flexing as he turned back to face me, a dry t-shirt in hand. Watching him toss it on might as well have been porn. I was hot and bothered by the whole thing.

Meanwhile, he was oblivious, canting his eyes my way as he walked to the kitchen. "Now for that tea," he said, his hand beckoning me to follow.

Next thing I knew, I was sitting at a small round table in the kitchen while he started a kettle. I couldn't quite believe that only minutes ago, I'd laid eyes on a man who'd haunted me from afar for too long. Miraculously, I'd completely forgotten about Joe when usually I'd be in a mental tailspin for a bit. I didn't know if Alex's crazy strong effect on me was a combination of my heightened state, or if it was just him. Either way, I welcomed the distraction he offered.

Alex was quiet for the several minutes until the tea kettle whistled. He poured two cups of tea and sat down opposite me, sliding one mug across the table. I curled my hands around it, savoring the warmth. His eyes landed on me, his chocolate gaze assessing. I felt suddenly self-conscious, masking it with a giant gulp of tea, completely forgetting that the water had just boiled moments ago and could've used a few minutes to cool. With a sputter, I spewed tea all over the table.

I looked up to find Alex's shoulders shaking slightly, his eyes glinting with mirth. "Bit too hot?" he asked with a low chuckle as he stood and stepped to the counter, returning to wipe the table with a paper towel. He handed me a clean one and tossed the other one in the trash can.

After I wiped my chin, I stood and dropped the wet paper towel in the trash.

Alex stood by the counter, his hands curled over the edge. "Need a dry shirt?" he asked, gesturing toward my shirt.

I glanced down and sighed. Wet splotches covered most of the front of my shirt. I was dressed in typical style this evening, jeans and a cotton shirt, this one a rich blue and fitted. I looked back up at Alex, trying not to blush, and shrugged. "Thanks for offering, but no need."

He barely nodded, his eyes locked to mine. The air hummed to life around us, and heat suffused me. All Alex had to do was look at me, and I wanted him. My nipples tightened, and it occurred to me it was probably quite obvious, seeing as my shirt was damp and sticking to my skin. I couldn't seem to move and stood there, maybe a foot or so away from Alex.

I wanted to step close to him again and feel his hard, muscled body against mine. I wanted to lose myself in the wild beat of this desire between us. *You have seriously lost it. Take a step back and think. You can't...*

My body, which suddenly seemed to have its own voice, loudly overrode my usual cautious, wise (or so I thought) voice. *Why? Why should you take a step back? The most delicious man you've ever kissed is standing right here in front of you. You know you can trust him.* Caution tried to make herself heard. *How do you know you can trust him?* This other side of me, driven by an overwhelming desire to explore every facet of the need Alex elicited, was quick to answer. *Because you know. He's Liam's best friend and so trustworthy Liam teases him about it. Aside from that, you can feel it. He's a rock, the good kind—strong, quiet and steady. Oh, and hot as hell. You finally have the chance you've been hoping for. Do something with it.*

I looked over at Alex, my mind lobbing points back and forth. At the moment, this emboldened voice, one that seemed borne solely out of my body's burning need for Alex, was definitely winning the debate. I wanted Alex. I wanted him badly.

I also wanted to banish the nightmares I'd been having for the last four years. They'd lessened in frequency and intensity, but they still happened every once in a while. I'd somehow gotten it in my head if I could find the right guy, I could have the fling to beat all flings and wrestle back control of my life. I hadn't had sex in four years for perfectly good reason, all things considered. Rape smashes desire with its fist. I'd begun to think maybe I wouldn't ever feel desire again. It was an odd sort of loss, an emptiness chased by anger. Anger that something had been stolen from me, maybe permanently. I wanted it back, to claim it as mine again.

Then came Alex. I'd watched him from a distance when I'd encounter him at gatherings with Olivia and Liam. He'd been tempting, but I hadn't spent any time with him, or gotten close enough to notice him the way I had last week. Only a few minutes alone with him and he'd shredded any worries I had about never experiencing desire again. I wanted to rip his clothes off and explore every inch of his perfect body. I wanted to see his eyes go dark again, his gaze so hot it made me wet just from a look.

Like now. His dark gaze held mine before his eyes dropped down. He might as well have touched my nipples. They tightened and stood at attention, aching to be uncovered. I wanted to lick him all over and wanted the same in return.

I stared back at him. I kept waiting for that feeling to come, the one I knew so well, where I got anxious inside, so anxious that I could hardly breathe and my chest felt as if it was about to be crushed from the weight of my fear. With Alex, that feeling didn't come. On nothing other than my gut and the knowledge that my dear friend's fiancée trusted this man implicitly, I trusted Alex completely.

The air around us was heavy now, reverberating with the beat of our desire. I held Alex's gaze as I closed the distance between us, stopping a whisper away from him. He tilted his head forward as I looked up.

"Harper, what are you...?"

"I want you," I said, my words coming out raspy. I spoke the raw truth because, well because when it came to Alex, it seemed that's all I had.

His eyes widened slightly. He stared at me, his gaze searching and darkening at once. I lifted a hand, because I couldn't help it, and traced along the edge of his strong jaw. His jaw tightened under my touch. His gaze went from hot to scorching, all the while he didn't say a word. My pulse had gone wild and I could hardly breathe. I traced down along his neck and over his chest, swallowing at the hard muscled planes under my palm. I wanted to feel his skin. So I did. I slipped my hand under his shirt and sighed at the feel of his skin—hot and smooth. His shirt bunched over my wrist as I pushed it up.

Alex suddenly moved, grabbing both of my hands fast in one of his large, strong hands. One easily held both of mine. My gaze had wandered down and slammed back into his. Dear God. If it was possible to get burned from a look, Alex's gaze almost did it. My skin prickled with awareness, and hot liquid need throbbed between my legs. A reckless feeling pushed at me. I was afraid he was going to make me stop, and I couldn't bear it. It felt so good to let something other than my cool intellect drive what was happening. It felt as if I was standing on the edge of a precipice, and I could either take control and fly into what was before me, or stay back, teetering on the edge and wondering what I might be missing.

In the grip of his hand, I fisted mine in his shirt and yanked him closer as I stepped flush against him.

"Harper."

His voice was edged with warning.

Heedless, I leaned up, tugging him further down to meet me. He didn't resist when he could've. He was stronger than me by a long shot. His lips were but a whisper away.

"What?" I asked.

Restless, I shifted my legs, feeling the moisture at the apex of my thighs when I did. His hot gaze held mine, searching and hungry at once. "What are you doing?" he bit out.

"I. Want. You." My words came out raspy,

but clear. Beyond feeling dizzy with need, I felt emboldened with Alex.

Shimmying one of my hands free from his grip, I slid it up around the nape of his neck. I could feel his heart pounding against the hand still held in his. His heart beat hard and fast, its rhythm solid and strong and imbuing me with more boldness. If I'd stopped to think right about now, I'd have lost it over what I was doing. But I wasn't thinking and I didn't want to. Well, it wasn't that I wasn't thinking at all—just that I was thinking only about one thing. Alex and more of the way I felt when I kissed him last week. It was such a relief not to feel controlled and cautious, that feeling alone was a bit of a rush. Throw in the most potent man I'd ever met, and I was on fire—inside and out.

After a heated moment, Alex leaned back incrementally. "Okay, but we're taking it slow," he said.

"Why?" I countered, almost annoyed at his high handedness.

His eyes darkened and one corner of his mouth curled up. "Because I don't like to rush."

A flash of uncertainty rose within. Before it had a chance to take over my thoughts, he closed the distance between us, fit his mouth over mine and promptly obliterated my senses. He freed my hand between us and slid his arms around me, lifting me high against him and turning to slide my hips on the counter. He gripped my bottom and pulled me flush against him, all the while kissing me fiercely—hot, wet, deep kisses. After the heated dive into our kiss, he drew back, his lips meandering in a slow path along the side of my neck where he nipped at my ear, sending shivers racing through me. A moan escaped, and I didn't care, heedless of anything but getting more.

My hands slipped under his shirt and up his back. I'd never noticed a man's back, but the feel of Alex's was heaven—every single inch of his was honed muscle, flexing under my touch. While I mapped my way around to his chest, his lips made their way along my collarbone and his hands traced up my sides under my shirt, his touch light as a feather and driving me wild. I arched my hips into his, sighing at the feel of his cock, hot and hard through the denim against me. I wanted everything, all at once now. I leaned back to say something. He lifted his head and his eyes collided with mine, his gaze so hot I shuddered. He hooked his hand under the edge of my shirt and lifted it off in one swift motion.

I heard it land on the tiled floor. The air whispered over my skin, the cool contrast to the heat inside sending a rush of goose bumps over its surface.

My breath came in shallow pants and my pulse skittered wildly. All he was doing was looking at me. That alone was so hot, my core throbbed and my hips arched reflexively against him, pleasure spiking through me. His eyes locked with mine, he trailed his fingers along the undersides of my breasts, my nipples tightening to the point of pain at the subtle touch.

I couldn't take it, this slow, teasing madness. I needed to barrel through this before I started thinking. I reached between us and started to unbutton his jeans.

In a flash, his hands were gripping mine. "Not now," he said, his words a gruff whisper.

"Why?" I asked, frustrated and impatient. I arched into him again and experienced a flash of satisfaction when his breath came out in a hiss.

"It's not about me tonight. Just you," he bit out.

My eyes swung back to his. I might not have had sex for four years, but I was no virgin. I'd dated here and there in college and was well aware most men had expectations, all of which involved them finding release somewhere in the course of whatever happened. I couldn't quite compute what he meant.

"What do you mean?"

My pause seemed to have given him just enough time to gain control again, and his words came out calmer and more measured. "Just that. It's all about you."

I still couldn't wrap my brain around what he meant. To be fair, I was caught in the tide of a lust so powerful, I could barely keep my head above water. With Alex's nearly perfect body pressed against mine and his hot gaze locked to mine, I couldn't think very well. At all. "I don't understand," I finally said.

"Let me show you," he said after another few beats where I contemplated whether it was actually possible to have an orgasm without touch. My panties were soaked and my channel was clenching. Every subtle shift of his cock against me—through my jeans and his—was so hot, I was teetering on the verge of release.

He flicked his thumb under the clasp of my bra and dipped his head to swirl his tongue over a nipple. It felt so good, so damn good, I cried out and gripped his hair. I tumbled into a blur of need and sensation as he proceeded to drive me wild, licking, sucking and nipping at my nipples. Awash in sensation, my hips were rolling into him when he drew my zipper down and slipped a hand over to cup my mound. Restless, I arched into him, a moaning sigh escaping when he dragged a finger back and forth over the wet silk of my underwear.

He trailed kisses up between my breasts and along the side of my neck before lifting his head.

"Harper."

At his gruff command, I dragged my eyes open and found his fiery gaze waiting.

I couldn't speak, so I simply stared at him, almost crying out when he hooked a finger under the edge of my panties and stroked through my folds. I was slick with need and teetering on the edge of a climax. My eyes started to fall closed.

"Look at me," he said. Again, his words were soft and gruff, yet his expectation was clear.

It was hard to look at him. The moment was overwhelming in ways I could barely comprehend. I hadn't been intimate in the slightest with anyone in four years. Before that...less than a half hour had wrecked my life, and I hadn't known if I'd ever dare to even think about sex again. Alex had already given me the gift of thinking about sex, but in the short week since our kiss, I hadn't know if I'd have the courage to go further. Yet, here we were. I wasn't afraid. In fact, I felt so comfortable with him, so abandoned in the desire between us, the comfort itself frightened me in a way. I hadn't expected this intimacy with him, this closeness where I wanted to lose myself in every moment with him.

"I want to see you come," he said.

His words hit me right in the heart. Just as he spoke, his slid a finger into my channel, knuckle deep. My climax rolled through me slowly, unraveling in spirals of pleasure and wracking me with shudders. Another finger joined the first—stroking in and out of my channel. It didn't take much—too long without letting go and in the grip of the fiercest desire I'd ever felt, I let go. Held in his dark gaze, the unraveling sped until I cried out, a sharp jolt of pleasure rocking me. My channel throbbed around his fingers. My head fell forward, thumping against his chest, as I tried to catch my breath.

I couldn't hear anything above the pounding of my heart for several moments. As my pulse finally slowed and my breathing returned to normal, actual thought entered my brain. What had I just done?

Um. Pretty obvious. You just had the best orgasm of your life at the hands of Alex Gordon, super sexy soccer star.

My snide side pointed out the incredibly obvious circumstances. Okay, when I'd been feeling bold and reckless, I wanted this. Actually, I wanted a lot more. Now, I felt exposed and vulnerable. I swallowed against the anxiety and uncertainty building inside and forced myself to focus on how I felt if I wasn't letting my brain churn. I felt...good. Really good. Alex had slid his hand out of my jeans and zipped them up sometime in the last few minutes. His head was bowed into the curve of my neck, and he was quiet. I could feel his cock—hard and hot—against me and wondered if he really meant it—that this time was only about me. I lifted my head and reached between us to drag my hand over his shaft. His head whipped up, his eyes locking to mine immediately.

"Harper."

The warning was there in his tone again.

I couldn't help it. He made me want to tease, so I cupped his cock through the denim and stroked up and down. His breath came out in a hiss, and he stepped back swiftly. Before I had a chance to speak, he erased the distance he'd just created between us, reaching up to hook my bra again. In a matter of seconds, he'd snagged my shirt off the floor and handed it to me. I was shaken enough—not the bad kind of shaken—that I simply put it on, wondering why he was holding back in seeking his own release when it was plainly obvious he was turned on.

He stood before me, his chiseled features tense. "Did you still want some tea?" he finally asked.

"I want to know why you're holding back." I was genuinely curious.

He was quiet for a few beats before he said, "Like I said, I don't like to rush."

I stared at him, so many questions tumbling through my thoughts I couldn't settle on any single one to ask.

"Don't go thinking this is a one-time thing. Trust me."

I did. Trust him, that is. Completely. He couldn't know how much that meant. The absolute confidence I had in my trust for him shook me for reasons I didn't dare to contemplate right now.

"Okay," I finally replied, battling with my internal disquiet.

I shimmied off the counter and straightened my clothes. "How about I take a rain check on that tea? I should probably get home."

"I'll walk you."

I almost automatically told him he didn't need to walk me home. Then, I realized I wanted him to. Badly. For reasons that had nothing to do with old nightmares and the man behind them. The man I'd seen before I came into Alex's apartment and whom I'd completely forgotten in the intervening time.

Alex walked me home, all the way up the stairs to my door. He waited until I was inside and then kissed me again. One kiss. One sweep of his tongue against mine. That's it, and I almost collapsed against the door after he left.

Chapter Five

ALEX

"Mate, you need to loosen up," Ethan said with a wink before he snagged a water bottle on the bench beside him and guzzled it.

I resisted the urge to glare at him and rolled my eyes instead. "And why is that?" I countered.

Ethan almost drained the water bottle before lowering it and glancing to me, swiping his sleeve across his face. We were at practice during a break for the defensive end while Coach worked with the offense. Ethan held my gaze for a moment before looking down as he idly swung the water bottle in a circle between his knees. "Ever since we lost last week, you've been damn serious. You're scaring the guys who don't know you as well."

I'd signed with the Seattle Stars along with three players from England—Liam, Ethan and Tristan. Tristan played offense alongside Liam, while Ethan played defense with me. We'd been here over a year now, but it was true that my mates from London knew me better. "Scaring them?" I asked in return.

"Yup. On your best days, you're quiet. I told the lads I didn't think you were too torn up over us losing. I've played with you before, so I know you know it comes with the game. I didn't tell 'em what I really think," he said with a sly grin.

I did glare at him now. "And what would that be?"

"Mate, you were all eyes for Harper the other night. I've never seen you look at a girl like that," he said, his grin stretching wider.

I couldn't help the laugh that rumbled from my chest. "And that has what to do with me looking too serious?"

Ethan, in typical low-key, teasing manner, winked. "She's got you all tied up. I've known you for years, mate. You hardly ever date. Oh, I know you had your arrangements back in London, but they were more like business than romance. The way you looked at Harper —that was something else. If you ask me, you need to have some fun. She might help you relax."

I stared at him and felt my jaw tightening. Damn if Ethan hadn't somehow zeroed in on exactly what was getting to me. I was beyond tied up in knots after the other night. I'd managed to walk Harper home and see her in without tearing her clothes off and sinking inside of her right there in the hallway outside her apartment, but my self-imposed control had come at a price. I'd been damn cranky ever since. I wasn't about to admit any of this to Ethan though. Not here and certainly not now.

Instead, I shrugged. "Maybe I like her. Otherwise, how about you lay off the amateur psychoanalysis?"

Ethan winked again and guzzled the last of the water, tossing the empty bottle into a recycling bin at the end of the bench. "Will do, mate." He stood and started to walk away before pausing to turn back. "Not that you're asking, but she's got it bad for you too."

I ran a hand through my hair and sighed, electing not to respond to Ethan's baiting. This was nothing new from him. Ethan wasn't one of those guys who drove me nuts with the way they treated women as another sport. Rather, he was a flirt who took flirting to great heights. He eschewed commitment and loved to tease. Now that Liam was engaged to Olivia, Ethan enjoyed teasing him about how quickly Liam had fallen. Liam was so far gone, he didn't even care.

My mind spun to Harper—reserved Harper who'd gone and blown my mind with her boldness the other night. I'd wanted to see behind to the other side of the invisible walls protecting her, and I had. When her gorgeous blue eyes held mine right as she started to come, her channel pulsing around my fingers...holy hell, I'd almost come in my jeans. Her quiet, controlled demeanor hid a woman of fierce passion.

Somehow I knew I still hadn't seen all of the layers fall away yet. I'd meant what I said when I told her I didn't want to rush. I never did, but there was more than that with her. I wanted more than a mutual exchange of pleasure with her. My mind flicked back to when we'd been standing out in the rain and that car pulled up to the stoplight. It hadn't been quite like when we'd been in the park and she'd almost frozen in place. But something flickered in her eyes. Then, she blew my mind and pushed me to the very edge of my control.

Cold showers and the mechanical release

I could give myself didn't assuage the need burning inside for her. Coach called my name, effectively snapping me out of my train of thought. As I walked back onto the pitch, I pondered when I'd see her again. She and Stanley had joined me for my morning run for the last two days, but she didn't speak of what passed between us the other night. Nor did I. I wouldn't wait much longer though. If anything, because I didn't know if I could.

"What do you think, Alex? Blue or green?" Liam asked, holding up a stationary card.

"Come again?" I countered, puzzled at his question.

Olivia had just walked by the kitchen table where I was sitting across from Liam and fanned a series of cards in front of him on the table. She hadn't said a word and kept on into the kitchen where she poured a glass of wine for herself and called over to us. "More beer, boys?"

Before I had a chance to reply to her, Liam did. "Two please," he called over his shoulder, his gaze swinging back to me. He lowered his voice. "Just tell me, blue or green.

These are our wedding invitations and she wants me to help pick the color."

I chuckled and reached across the table, sliding the cards closer to me. They each had sample text in different fonts and two colors. "Blue. Definitely blue." Instantly Harper's gorgeous eyes came to mind. I'd almost taken her against a tree this morning. That's how bad it was getting. She was meeting me every morning, yet those walls had gone back up, stronger than ever. I shoved my thoughts off of her and onto the topic of Liam and Olivia's wedding invitations. "Think you're supposed to pick the font too, mate."

Liam's eyes whipped to mine, just as Olivia reached the table and set down two beers. She looked between us, her green gaze assessing. At a glance, it had surprised me that Liam fell for her. She was beautiful, no doubt about that, but not the usual fun-loving, casual women Liam had dated before he met her. Olivia kept her dark curls tied up in a bun most of the time and wore glasses. At first blush, she was all business. With Liam, she was as bad off as he was. Half the time, I was reminding them they weren't alone. I was beyond pleased Liam had found her. He'd had a rough year before we signed with the Stars. His mum died of a stroke, and he was distracted enough that he lost his touch in play and our team in London lost a crucial game as a result. Meeting Olivia had tugged him out of the fog of his grief.

Olivia looked from me to Liam. "As usual, Alex is paying better attention. I need to know what font you like too. Not just the color," she said with a feigned sigh.

Liam met my gaze and rolled his eyes. "Right then." He glanced up to Olivia, slipped his arms about her waist and pulled her into his lap. "That's why he's my best mate. He's all about the details."

Olivia flushed pink when Liam brazenly kissed his way down her neck. She wiggled off of his lap. "Good grief! I can't go anywhere with you."

"We're at home!" Liam protested.

Olivia shook her head and bestowed a flustered smile on me. "Alex has great judgment. If he thinks blue looks best, we'll do that. Which font do you like?" she asked me next.

After a few moments of back and forth over the fonts with them, Olivia scooped up the cards and returned them to a stack on the corner of the kitchen counter before joining us at the table. She chatted about her day and then looked to me. "So I heard you've been going running with Harper."

Her statement was an abrupt change of topic. For a moment, I was flummoxed. After a beat, I nodded. "I have."

I toyed with asking Olivia about Harper, but I wasn't sure what I wanted to ask. Well, that didn't quite cut it. I wanted to know *everything* about Harper, but worried that might reveal how powerfully I was drawn to her.

Olivia looked at me for a long moment, her eyes considering. "Good."

I sensed something lay behind her comment, but hell if I knew what. "If you don't mind me asking, why would you care if I'm running with Harper?"

Olivia traced a circle around the base of her wineglass before shrugging, as if to herself. "Well, you'll either hear it from me or someone else. Harper hasn't gone running outside for a few years. You probably didn't know, but she was a track star in college. She ran cross country and was ranked nationally."

I could've guessed something like that. Harper easily kept pace with me and ran as if she had for many years. I didn't know why this mattered though. "Right. So...?"

"Well, it all fell apart when we were seniors in college. She got raped by a guy from another university. Even worse, it happened when she was out running on campus. It was all over the news. It's not like she tries to keep it a secret, but it's not like she likes to talk about it either," Olivia said softly.

Olivia's words hit me like a bolt of lightning, so hard I reeled inside. Someone raped Harper? Bloody hell. On the heels of my shock came fury, raw and cold. I wanted to race out of here and find the man who hurt her and inflict the same level of horror upon him. That's not to say I wanted to rape the guy, but beating him senseless might, just might, suffice. In the few seconds that passed since Olivia had dropped this little bomb, I forgot all about trying to keep my feelings for Harper masked. It wasn't that I cared all that much what Liam knew. More that I wanted time to feel things out and see where they went. I was hyperaware of how easy it was to have the media sniffing at my heels. It had been slightly better since we were in the US. Football in Britain, well pretty much anywhere else in the world, was revered. Players were dogged by the local media back there. I'd managed to avoid the attention then and hoped to keep doing so now.

Whatever showed on my face nudged

Liam to straighten in his chair, his eyes narrowing. I shackled the fury inside and looked at Olivia. "What the hell? Who is he?" I demanded.

Olivia's eyes widened before her expression softened. "Alex, she's fine. It was four years ago. It won't do her a bit of good for you to get all riled up over this." She glanced to Liam. "You didn't tell him?" she asked him.

Liam's watchful gaze caught mine before swinging to Olivia. "No. It's not like we talk much about your friends. Not to mention it's a bloody shitty topic. It's awful what happened," he replied before looking back to me. "It pisses me off too, mate, but ease up."

I could tell he was trying to suss out what was up with me. I'd be pissed to hear about any woman getting hurt in any way. But this was Harper. In a matter of weeks, my curiosity about her had gone from simply that to far more. I was relieved with Liam's next comment.

"I told you, luv. Alex would protect the whole wide world if he could. He's a beast like that. Remember how I told you he was worried about you when we started dating? Hearing one of your friends got raped is like that times a million," Liam said.

About now, he'd usually grin, but this

wasn't funny. Nothing about rape was funny. I ran a hand through my hair and took a long drag off my beer. I bloody well didn't like being this furious without a target. My mind spun back to the day I'd encountered Harper in the park, the very day she'd first kissed me a bit later. I couldn't help but wonder if the man we'd seen had been the very man who raped her.

Looking to Olivia, I asked, "What happened to the guy?"

Her gaze darkened and her mouth tightened, anger and resignation evident on her face. "Well, see, he was a track star too. He attended a different university, but it was right here in Seattle. Harper doesn't hide what happened if anyone happens to ask, but she's never talked much about the details since right after it happened. I know more from the papers than I know from her. I don't think it will help you to get angry about something you can't do anything about."

"Tell me what happened," I said, trying to keep the anger out of my tone. I wasn't angry with Olivia, but bloody hell I needed to know what happened to the guy.

Her eyes flicked to Liam.

"Luv, just tell him what you know. If you don't, Alex will track the details down on his own, so you might as well save him the trouble," Liam said.

Bloody right he was. As it stood, I'd be on the guy's scent as soon as I could.

Olivia took a gulp of wine and eyed me. "You're a good man, Alex Gordon," she said softly.

I took another long drag off my beer and circled my hand in the air. "Right, right. Carry on and tell me what happened to the bastard."

"He was arrested and charged, but he got a good attorney and fought like hell. In the end, the charges were pleaded down. I'd have to look up the details on that. He served two months in jail and was released. He didn't even have to register as a sex offender." She shook her head furiously at that, her eyes bright with tears. "Harper's one of my best friends. What he did was horrible, and in the end, it was hardly a speed bump for him. He got kicked off the team, but he still got to graduate."

"Where is he now?" I asked, my focus like a laser on the present.

Olivia gulped in air and let it out in a heavy sigh. "He works at some finance place in Seattle. I try to keep tabs on him. Since he doesn't have to register as a sex offender, I don't know where he lives, and he does a pretty good job of keeping his online profile to a minimum."

"Who is he?"

Liam stayed quiet, but I could tell he sensed my fury.

"His name is Joe Schmidt," Olivia said, her worried gaze scanning my face. "Promise me you won't try to do anything. There's nothing to do. He was charged and convicted on whatever dumb charges they agreed on. The whole investigation ruined Harper's life for a while. She was miserable, and it was just awful. She's moved on. I mean, I wondered if she'd ever run outside again and now she's running with you. That's why I'm happy about that, but I get why you're pissed. Trust me, every time I think about it, I want to scream. But let Harper stay moved on. Please."

Olivia's gentle words penetrated the fury coiling inside. I closed my eyes and took a slow breath, I hadn't realized I was clenching a fist. I eased my grip and leaned back in my chair, opening my eyes to find two concerned gazes on me. "Right. I know you're right," I said, directing my words to Olivia. "Doesn't change the fact it bloody sucks. It's bollocks the guy spent only two months in jail. How bad…" I forced myself to stop with the questions. I'd save them for another time, or find the answers myself.

Olivia reached over and squeezed my hand. "You see Harper as she is now. She's strong and healthy and fine. She's really, really fine. There's only one other thing I'd wish for her."

"What's that?" I asked, my question reflexive.

"I want her to find someone. She hasn't even gone on a date since it happened. She's so awesome, but I don't know if she even thinks about it." Olivia glanced between us. "I mean, right? She's pretty and smart and funny and…"

Liam reached over and caught Olivia's hand in his, lifting it for a kiss. "Of course she is. But I think you're going to have to let this ball stay in Harper's court."

Meanwhile, I sat there stunned, my mind spinning over the revelations and wondering just what to think about what happened between Harper and me.

Chapter Six

HARPER

I jogged down the stairs to the front door of my building with Stanley at my side. It was a small thing, but I loved how the stairs curved along the wall. It always felt as if I was spinning slowly down a slide and out the front door. I had a little buzz of joy inside, knowing I was about to walk out and meet Alex for another run. After he'd invited me to run with him in the mornings, I'd quickly fallen into a pattern of meeting him daily. Unbeknownst to him, his offer had given me a small gift. I used to run outside all the time, hours upon hours every week. In a blink, I lost the joy of it after an early morning run in that time where the light hadn't quite washed away the darkness. Crossing paths with Joe at that in between time had ripped my joy away. Joe who seemed to live somewhere nearby. Joe whose mere presence should've permanently scared me away from returning to the park.

I hated knowing he was near, but I felt safe with Alex and I'd missed running so. Alex had stirred deep waters in me. He made me think I could steal back what had been stolen from me. It wasn't just the fact he made me so hot I forgot I'd once thought I'd never want to have sex again. He made me think maybe I could banish the hold Joe had on me. The fact I was running outside at all was a small miracle. I'd never stopped running, but I'd relegated myself to a treadmill. Even though the mechanics were close enough, I'd dearly missed the joy and invigoration of the fresh early morning air and watching the sunrise.

I reached the entryway and glanced to Stanley. His blue eyes met mine, and he nudged my hand with his nose. Stanley loved running too. It was safe to say he adored Alex and had come to expect our morning runs now. He pressed his nose to one of the small windowpanes along the side of the door. A glance outside told me Alex wasn't here yet. I was looking down at my watch when Stanley let out a soft woof. Just as I wondered what he was reacting to, Alex strolled into view.

My breath hitched and my belly clenched. Damn. He was so ridiculously handsome. With his apartment east of mine, the sun was rising behind him, glinting off his dark brown hair. He walked with an easiness, emanating strength and masculine grace. Every inch of him was muscled and mouth-watering. It had been over a week since he'd practically left me in a puddle by my door. Too long. I was determined to push him past his ridiculous edge of control, but I'd yet to finagle an opportunity. Today was Saturday though, and I knew we'd be in the same place tonight. Olivia had invited me to dinner with her and Liam and said she needed some girl back up since Liam's friends would be there.

That little buzz of joy propelled me through the door and down the steps with Stanley padding along at my side. Alex stopped at the foot of the stairs just as I reached the bottom step. His brown eyes met mine, the intensity of his gaze giving me pause. His eyes swept over me, sending a jolt through me. When he met my gaze again, I was confused. He felt coiled tight and had lines of tension bracketing his face. Even in rest, he was an intense man, but at the moment, I was taken aback. My first instinct was to want to comfort him and before I realized it, I'd reached out and slid my hand down his arm.

"Are you okay?" I asked when he didn't say anything for a moment.

He gave his head a small shake when Stanley stepped to his side and nudged his hand. Alex stroked Stanley, his hand sliding in a path along the center of Stanley's back. He'd quickly come to know what Stanley loved and commenced to idly scratch between Stanley's shoulders. Alex looked back up at me. "I'm fine. You?"

Whatever tension he'd been holding eased. His eyes softened as he looked at me. I took a breath and the knot of tension I hadn't noticed dissolved. "Ready to run," I replied.

He held my gaze for a few more beats, his eyes searching. For what, I didn't know. "Okay then. Let's go." He glanced to Stanley. "Ready Stanley?"

Stanley simply nudged Alex's leg with his gray head. At that, we started jogging. It

worked out that the distance from my apartment to the park was just enough to warm us
up. By the time we jogged through the park
entrance, we were ready to pick up the pace.
We didn't talk much while we ran, which
suited me fine. Alex's pace was strong and
steady. Aside from the layers of reasons why I
enjoyed running with him, he was nearly perfect as a running partner for me. He could
easily hold pace and his stamina was excellent. Given that he was a professional soccer
player, this wasn't surprising, but nevertheless
I appreciated it.

We ran through the wooded portion of
the park and down to a pathway that offered
a view of Puget Sound. Gulls called and a
salty breeze gusted off the water. The old
runner's high that I loved rose inside, something I'd never quite felt when I ran on a
treadmill. Whether it was a myth or not, I
loved the rush of adrenaline and the soft ex-
hilaration I felt when I ran through the cool
morning air. It had rained during the night,
so the air was earthy and felt as if it had been
washed clean by the rain. Sun glittered on the
damp leaves and grass.

Stanley ran on one side of me with Alex
on the other, his footfalls steady and even. I

felt strong this morning as we crested a small rise and turned a corner on the path. I was looking out toward the water when I sensed Alex go tense. I glanced to his face to see those tight lines again, his eyes dark. I followed his gaze to see Joe Schmidt, my personal hell, running in the distance. That sick feeling of dread coiled in my gut, but I pushed back against it. It had been four years since Joe raped me. He'd done a measly two months in jail, and I'd moved on as best I could. I was determined not to let his presence ruin what I'd found again. I swallowed against the fear and kept running. I felt half-sick and ready to vomit, but if I was ever going to get past this awful feeling, I could do it with Stanley and Alex.

Alex slowed his pace and glanced to me. "Let's take a different route today."

I didn't know how, but in a flash I realized he knew I'd been raped and that Joe was the man responsible. I stopped abruptly, a wild feeling coursing through me—fear mixed with dread mixed with adrenaline mixed with a dose of recklessness.

"Why?"

Joe was still a good distance away, but his stride kept moving in our direction. Alex met my gaze, his own expression a mix of anger and frustration. "Because," he bit out.

"Who told you?" I asked.

Alex's eyes widened. He rested a hand on his hip, his breath coming in heaves. "Harper... Bloody hell. Can we talk about this later?"

Neither one of us was saying aloud what we were talking about, but it was clear. "We can talk later, but we're not taking a different route."

My tone was mulish, and most of me thought I was crazy. Completely off my rocker, in fact. *You don't have to get comfy with seeing Joe. He raped you. Getting past it doesn't mean getting okay around him.* That voice was insistent and quite rational. Yet, I was in a strange place right now. I didn't want to bend my life into contortions to avoid Joe. I'd been doing that for four years. I perversely wanted him to know I didn't give a damn and I wasn't afraid. I had nothing to lose because he'd already smashed my life to smithereens once. He couldn't do it again. Plus, I had Alex with me. I knew I was safe with him.

Alex leaned his head back to stare at the sky before lasering me with his dark gaze again. "Unless you want me to beat him senseless right now, we'd best take another route," he said flatly.

I had no idea how Alex pieced together who Joe was, but I knew without a doubt that if I insisted we cross paths with Joe, Alex would probably do just as he said. As it was, his fists were clenched and his face dark with anger. Alex, who was almost always calm, who felt like a rock of safety to me, felt dangerous right now. Not dangerous to me, but most definitely dangerous to Joe. Much as a part of me wouldn't mind seeing Joe get his ass kicked, that wasn't what I wanted right now. I looked back at Alex, a rush of emotion welling inside of me. I fought to keep from crying and couldn't say if they were good tears or bad tears. Maybe both. I finally nodded in assent and started running again, following Alex's lead as he turned up another path.

I could feel the coiled energy coming off of Alex in waves as we ran and didn't quite know what to do about any of it. The facts of my rape were no secret to anyone who knew me, or anyone who happened to be in Seattle at the time of the rape. It was all over the news because I'd been a track star at University of Washington, and Joe had been one at another nearby university. Looking back, I occasionally wondered how I'd had the courage to report the rape. In hindsight, I think it was because I'd been raised to believe things worked out how they should. People did bad things, you told the police, and they made it right. Little did I know it was never that simple when it came to rape.

Joe had jogged by me in the semi-darkness that morning. I'd recognized him because he was one of a number of runners who frequented the university grounds. Another pass by him and the rest was a jumble of awful in my memory. What was sharp was how I felt afterwards—shattered inside and out.

I had no sense of how much time passed before I climbed to my feet and numbly walked to the police station. Thus began months of hell. To this day, I recognized I should feel lucky to have seen any legal consequences at all. I was sadly unable to avoid reading about the recent spate of news stories about college sexual assault and the usual weak response from universities. I hadn't known at the time that it was smart to have gone to the city police first. I only went there because it was closer, no other reason. There was DNA and physical evidence of his assault. Even with all of that, the prosecutor had offered a plea deal because Joe had an aggressive defense attorney who submitted reams upon reams of court filings to slow the proceedings down, and Joe argued it was consensual—as if leaving someone badly bruised and battered was consensual. Joe managed to graduate before the plea deal was finalized.

After those grueling, awful months, I'd wanted nothing more than to forget everything that happened. It had taken me four years to get to where I was now, a place where I mostly felt at peace. My mind spun over how Alex might've sorted out this part of my past. It wasn't that I wanted to keep it secret. No, that was impossible. It's just it would've been nice not to be seen as a victim in Alex's eyes. I didn't want anyone's pity. Most certainly not that of the first man who'd made me feel alive inside in years, made me think maybe, just maybe, I could take back something I'd thought lost.

We ran through the forest, the sunlight falling through the trees in shafts. Within another few moments, we were back on the sidewalk and jogging to the steps of my apartment building. Alex came to a stop and rested his hands on his hips. He looked over at me, his dark gaze searching my face. In the weeks since we'd been running together, this was the time when he usually said goodbye and waited until I let myself in the door. He always waited until the door closed behind me. Right now, I didn't want him to leave. Which was crazy. I didn't want to talk about Joe or any of the mess I imagined Alex thought we needed to talk about. No, rather I felt driven and reckless. I wanted all of this with Alex to stay pure, to not be sullied by an event four years that had been like a wrecking ball in my life. It felt as if that wrecking ball was swinging its way into my future, and I didn't like it.

I didn't know why, but with Alex, my body took over, rather insistently in fact. Intellectually, I thought I should be so rattled at seeing Joe again that the last thing on my mind would be anything even remotely resembling sex. But Joe was long gone in my mind. Alex stood before me. His t-shirt was damp from his sweat and clung to his muscled chest. Heat coiled low in my belly, and I wanted nothing but him.

"Do you want some tea?" I blurted out, the only question I could think of. I'd usually have a cup of coffee after a shower, but I thought Alex preferred tea.

His eyes widened slightly before he looked up to the sky again. His gaze leveled with mine after another moment, and he nodded. "Don't suppose you have coffee?"

I didn't wait and walked up the stairs, my body humming. "Of course I have coffee. I just thought you were a tea guy," I said as he followed me inside and up the stairs with Stanley right behind us.

Chapter Seven

ALEX

I splashed icy water on my face and wiped it dry with a towel. Carefully hanging the towel on its hook by the sink, I stared at myself for a moment. My hair stuck up in spikes, as it tended to do after a run. My t-shirt was damp. I tried to ascertain if I looked as angry as I felt. Seeing Joe Schmidt had sent me to a place inside I hadn't been in years. If Harper hadn't been with me, I would've run straight at him and clocked him. But she had been, and I hadn't wanted to rattle her in any way. I'd seen the man I now knew to be Joe enough times in the park that I knew I'd best him in a fight. It wouldn't be much trouble really, and it would feel so damn good. Ever since I'd spoken to Olivia and Liam yesterday, I'd been wanting to.

I was known for never losing my cool on the field, and I didn't. My nerves were hard won. I'd been raised in a middle class town outside of London—a lovely town in the English countryside. My father had been a barrister. On its face, his life was proper. Behind closed doors, he wielded power with the threat of violence toward my mum, my two sisters and me. He rarely used violence, but when he did the message was clear—violence was the consequence if you didn't toe his line. I'd been a rough lad, lashing out the only way I'd learned. Then, I'd lucked into landing on a football team with Liam when I was eight years old. I loved it. My dad let me play because he liked the prestige that came with having a boy who was one of the best footballers in town. I lucked into finding a few men I could look up to who weren't my father and learned violence wasn't the only way to solve problems.

I didn't even have to try all that hard to manage my temper. But it was there, deep under the surface. Very few things caused the tail of my temper to flick. Violence against anyone vulnerable would do it. Raping a woman I'd come to care way too much about in a very short time—well, to say that lit my fuse was a massive understatement.

Yet, reverberating in my thoughts was how absolutely critical it was I didn't lose control. Harper didn't need to see that. No matter how much Joe deserved it. I couldn't suss out how Harper was doing. She felt jumpy and restless when we walked into her apartment. I'd asked to use the loo to catch my breath and because I hoped a splash of icy water would cool the anger inside. It helped, but I still wanted to make this right for Harper.

Olivia said to let Harper be with this. Don't make this a battle when it isn't for her.

I was trying to make sense of what to do, but I simply didn't know if I could just let this sit. It wasn't right. Yet, what Harper wanted had to be what happened. I pushed through the door and returned to the kitchen. The scent of coffee filtered through the air. Harper was rinsing something in the sink. Stanley had stretched out in a patch of sunshine in the living room and was already sound asleep. After turning the water off, she dried her hands and shifted to face me, leaning her hips against the counter.

"Coffee's almost ready," she said.

I nodded and tried to shove the questions

I had about what must be a hellish topic for her out of my mind. She crossed her arms and tapped the toe of one foot lightly on the floor. After a moment of silence, she gestured to the island between the kitchen and living room where there were low stools. "You can sit if you'd like."

I hooked a hand over the back of one of the stools and sat, resting an elbow on the counter and wondering what mundane topic we could discuss. It all felt ridiculous. I might only be just getting to know Harper beyond the superficial, but it didn't feel right to try to ignore what had happened and to pretend I didn't know about her past. I ran a hand through my hair and leaned back.

"Would you like me to answer your question in the park?" I finally asked in reference to her question about who told me about Joe. I figured it was best to give her the chance to decide if we talked about anything related to the last fifteen minutes or so.

Her eyes widened slightly, and she tightened her arms where they crossed. For a flash, I saw that guarded quality she carried with her, but then she took a deep breath and let it out with a sigh. "I'm guessing Olivia told you," she finally said, her voice soft and edged with weariness.

"Right. She wasn't trying to gossip. I think she was trying to be helpful," I offered, not ready to admit I'd demanded it from Olivia when she made her passing comment about Harper running with me.

"I know. Most everyone I know and plenty of strangers know what happened. It's not a big secret in my life. I guess I was a little startled you figured out who Joe was."

I watched her and held myself back from standing and wrapping her in my arms. It took an enormous amount of restraint, but I managed. I sensed she didn't want to be viewed as vulnerable.

"Right. After Olivia told me what happened, I looked him up. Maybe it's none of my business, but..."

But what? What was I doing looking up the guy? The quick answer was I wanted to make sure I knew precisely who hurt Harper. My gut had told me it would be the very man we'd encountered in the park before, and my gut had been right. I'd seen Joe's photo online and recognized him immediately.

Harper was still waiting for me to fin-ish, her blue eyes watching and waiting pa-tiently. I shifted my shoulders just as the coffee maker beeped. Harper didn't turn away, so I took a breath and plowed ahead. Maybe I wasn't comfortable with any of this, but she was asking, so I'd answer. "I wanted to know who he was. After the other morning when we saw him, well...I was worried. I'm not trying to dredge anything up. I just..." I lifted my hands and let them fall. "Hell, I don't know. All I can say is I figured I'd rather know who the guy was in case I ever saw him."

Harper nodded, chewing the inside of her cheek as she did. After a moment, she turned and poured two cups of coffee before sitting down beside me. The island counter curved such that we were angled toward each other. She slid a cup of coffee in front of me. "Cream or sugar?" she asked.

"Neither," I said before taking a gulp. The rich, slightly bitter flavor hit me, and I closed my eyes.

"I guess I should say thanks for caring enough to want to look the guy up," Harper said, her words soft, but laced with anger.

Opening my eyes, I looked over to find her staring into her mug as she circled it in her hand.

"The whole thing's bloody awful. Now I know who he is, if I see him..." My words trailed off because I didn't think it would be particularly helpful to tell her I'd be happy to bash his face in.

"You can beat him senseless?" she said, an odd, sad smile curling her lips as she repeated my earlier words.

I shrugged and took another swallow of coffee. "Yup. If needed, that's what I'll do." I set my mug down and looked over at her. "But if you told me not to, I'd leave him alone. You have to know that."

She stopped circling her mug in her hands, her eyes whipping up to mine. I could feel her searching me. The air was taut around us, humming with the intensity I'd come to recognize whenever I was near her. At the moment, it wasn't weighted with desire, but a simple depth of feeling.

She finally nodded slowly. "That's good to know." She paused, chewing the inside of her cheek again as she eyed me. "If you want to know the truth, part of me would love for you to kick his ass. The other part of me knows it's not worth it. He's not worth any of it, and it won't change what happened." Another long pause. This time, she drummed her fingers on the counter and took a gulp of coffee. "I guess it's weird to say this, but I'm glad you looked him up. I try not to think about him too much because it's been four years. I only moved into this apartment a few months ago, and I didn't know he lived anywhere near here. I don't like to worry my friends and family, so I haven't told anyone I saw him. I guess it makes me feel better knowing you know he's around. In a roundabout way, I think I'm saying thanks," she said with a small smile, her dimple winking at me.

I absorbed her words and her smile, and my chest felt tight. I was used to worrying about people. I'd spent my entire childhood worrying about my mum and my two sisters. Whenever I looked back, I remembered the sense of freedom I felt when I played football. It was about the only thing I could do to escape the house and the heaviness that resided there. Funny thing, but I'd never worried about my own safety. My dad was the kind of jerk who steered clear of anyone who could push back too hard, so aside from verbal attacks, he largely left me alone. Even when I wasn't very big, I didn't hesitate to lash back. By the time I was in my teens, I was bigger, taller and stronger than him. Only then did he back off from my mum and my sisters. I'd had it in the back of my mind to talk my mum into moving out before I left for university, but he died from a heart attack and that was that. My sense of relief had been profound and only sadness had followed.

I looked to Harper and wondered if I could stop worrying about her. I didn't think so. It came too easily to me. Plus, she didn't need to do this alone. I wanted to demand she tell Olivia and Daisy and anyone else who cared about her that Joe was nearby. My mind snapped at me, reminding me this had to be hers to handle. The last thing she needed was me taking control and dictating how she should deal with the bloody hellish reality of accidentally moving into a neighborhood where the man who once raped her happened to frequent.

I took a swallow of my coffee and belatedly nodded. "No thanks needed," I finally replied.

A horn honked from the street. The sun falling through Harper's front windows glinted on her hair. She idly traced a pattern along the edges of the tiled counter while I wondered what to say next.

"Can we talk about something else?" she asked suddenly.

"Whatever you want."

Her eyes brightened. She nibbled on her

bottom lip as she looked over at me, re-minding me of how good her lips felt.

Mate, what are you thinking? Not supposed to think about anything like that right now.

I gave a mental shake. Hell, I didn't know if it was proper to think about her like that at all. My mind spun to the day she'd kissed me —so boldly—and then skipped ahead to the feel of her channel clenching around my fingers. I didn't know what to think of any of that now.

I jumped when she slid her hand onto my leg. We were seated quite close. When my eyes whipped up, hers were right there—bright blue and flashing with something I didn't quite know how to read.

I took another gulp of my coffee, buying a moment to gather myself. My body had tight-ened, electricity spinning through it the mo-ment she touched me. Because that's the effect Harper had on me. Fuck. My mind was definitely in a different place than my body and prepared for an all out internal lecture to keep me from doing something stupid.

I stared at Harper, trying to read into her gaze. Her eyes darkened. "Is this a thing where you get all weirded out because, well, because of this morning?" she demanded, her eyes snapping.

Bloody hell. I'd conveniently blanked out how assertive she could be and certainly didn't expect her to get pissed at me. Saying nothing wouldn't help. "Don't think I'm acting weird. It's been, well, I suppose it's been an odd morning. That's all."

Harper kept me in her sights, a flush cresting her cheeks. "Don't you dare let the past mess this up." Her words were fierce, her flush deepening as she spoke.

I was truly torn inside. My body, well, my body wanted to yank her to me. A vision of her straddling my lap flashed through my mind, and my cock twitched. All the while, my mind was trying to pump the brakes. Big time. I didn't know if there was a right way to go about any of this, but...

My thoughts came to a screeching halt when Harper stood abruptly. Seated on the stool, my knees were splayed with my feet hooked on the footrest. She stepped between my knees, her sudden closeness sending a bolt of need through me. With me seated, our faces were level, and she was but a whisper away. Bloody hell. She could *not*...

Mid-thought, she lifted a hand and ran it through my messy hair. See, she touched me and my usual control vanished. My heart beat hard and fast against my ribs. Her eyes scanned my face, the blue darkening to navy. I forced myself to hold still, tension vibrating through my body. Her hand sifted through my hair and trailed down my cheek before she tilted forward and brought her lips to mine. Later, I'd wonder about her boldness because I was usually the one to initiate when it came to women, mostly because I liked to be in control. With Harper, the only control I'd held to was not letting her push this too far and too fast.

In this moment with her plump lips warm against mine, I didn't wonder about anything. I turned the tables and yanked her to me, sweeping my tongue in her mouth. She gasped and then dove into our kiss as if her life depended on it. Our tongues tangled while her hands mapped my chest. I was on fire, inside and out, so hot for her, I could hardly contain it. She felt so good, so fucking good against me, her lush curves and fit body delicious in contrast. My lips blazed a trail of kisses down her neck, the skin soft and tangy. In the midst of our heated kiss, my phone went off, blaring out the chorus from All You Need is Love by the Beatles, courtesy of Liam who'd put it on my phone over a year ago. I'd never bothered to change it.

The repeat of the chorus nudged me into

sanity. I couldn't quite bring my lips off of her skin—it was too delicious—but I stopped in my meanderings and held still. I could feel the pounding of her heart, my own beating in a rough percussive rhythm along with hers. My cock was so hard it bordered on painful. I forced myself to lift my head, instantly missing the taste of her skin.

She looked as gobsmacked as I felt. The reckless wildness I'd sensed from her was tempered, but just barely. Over the pounding of my heart, I forced myself to speak, scrambling inside for some semblance of control. "I didn't mean..."

"Don't you dare tell me you didn't mean that," she said, her voice low and her words heated.

"That's not what I was about to say."

I took a shuddering breath, grasping for control. My hold on it was so weak as to be useless, but I hung on. I leaned back slightly, needing to create some space between us even if it was infinitesimal. "I didn't mean for that to get out of hand," I finally added.

Harper's eyes flashed again, but she was quiet. My mind was jumbled. There was the ever-present pounding need to just forget everything else and lose myself in Harper. Underneath that layer was the bubbling awareness that Harper wasn't the kind of woman I typically sought out. She wasn't a woman looking for nothing more than a tidy arrangement to meet purely physical needs. The connection between us was magnetic, and I could hardly keep from avoiding its pull. All of that existed before I'd known a thing about one event in her past, an event that loomed far larger than I wished. I'd meant not to rush before knowing a thing about her past. I sensed she'd be furious if I said aloud that knowing what I knew now changed things. Yet, it did. I didn't know what she sought from me. I didn't know how to square her boldness with her past. I wanted to sort out all of this before things went further, yet I imagined Harper would be beyond angry if I spoke any of this aloud.

I eased my hands away—one had slid up her back and the other to cup her bottom. That hand wanted to stay right where it was, cupping her lush bottom and savoring her softness. I forced it to move, an act of will and immense discipline. I stroked both palms down her arms and looked deep into her eyes. "The thing is, I can't kiss you without it getting out of hand bloody fast. Nothing about today or anything Olivia told me changes the fact I already told you I didn't want to rush things."

She stared back at me, her intent gaze softening. I hadn't thought ahead about my words, but they seemed to ease that reckless, angry edge to her. After a beat, she nodded. "You did," she said, her words falling into the room softly.

She bit her lip, a slow smile spreading. Her smile just about made my day. Her whole face transformed, that dimple winking, her eyes tilting up at the corners, and an almost sneaky glint of mirth in her eyes appearing. She didn't dole out smiles often, so they were all the more special. She stepped back, and damn if I didn't want to yank her back to me. My cock throbbed and I didn't want to lose the feel of her warmth and softness. I had to remind myself of what I'd just said and why.

Long game, mate. That's what you're after.

"Will you be at dinner tonight?" Harper asked.

"Huh?"

Her smile stretched wider, and she reached for her coffee, taking a sip before she replied. "Dinner with Liam and Olivia."

"Right. Of course. You?"

Liam asked me to meet him, so I'd be there. That's the kind of mates we were.

"I'll be there. Do you want to walk together?"

Being a guy, I hadn't even considered that if Liam asked me to be somewhere, it was highly likely Olivia had asked the same of her friends. I was unaccountably pleased to realize Harper would be there. "Shall I meet you here?"

She nodded and turned to refill her coffee. I discreetly adjusted my shorts and stood. "I should go. I could use a shower."

She spun to face me. For a moment, it looked as if she meant so say something of import, but then she gave her head a little shake and nodded. "Okay. I'll see you later then."

I walked to the door. Just as I was opening it, she spoke. "All You Need is Love?"

At a glance, I saw her shoulders shaking with her laugh. I shrugged. "Liam's doing."

Chapter Eight

HARPER

"What?!" Daisy exclaimed, her brown eyes wide.

I nodded and endeavored to keep from laughing. Olivia and Daisy were my closest friends. Olivia tended toward being more serious, and until she met Liam, she had lived and breathed her work as an orthopedic surgeon. Daisy had also gone into medicine, however she was a researcher. Of the three of us, Daisy was definitely the clown. At the moment, she was goggling at me because I'd just told her I'd decided I planned to break my years long drought of no sex with Alex. Daisy wasn't easy to surprise, so I was savoring the moment.

She opened her mouth to say something and then left it hanging open.

I grinned. "Wow. It's more fun to surprise you than I thought. I'll have to try a little harder to make it happen."

Daisy snapped her mouth shut and gave her head a shake, her blonde hair swinging back and forth. "Oh hon. It's gonna be years before you top this." She held a finger up and paused to take a gulp of coffee.

We were meeting at Desert Isle Coffee, a favorite hangout of ours. Up until my recent move, I rarely made it over, but now I lived on the same side of town. Desert Isle was named as such because it was a respite from the typical cool, damp days of Seattle. It was always warm and dry and had amazing coffee. After Alex had left this morning, I'd called up Daisy and Olivia. I needed some girl time. Olivia had been busy, but Daisy was here. Daisy was like a ray of sun—in looks and personality. With her blonde locks, wide brown eyes and curvy figure, she was plain gorgeous. She was also funny as hell and direct to the point of ridiculous sometimes.

Daisy set her coffee down and angled her head to the side. "Let me get this right: you're making a play for Alex Gordon and it's just for sex. Did I hear you correctly?" Daisy said, her eyes still wide with disbelief.

I nodded and ignored the little skip in my heartbeat. It seemed like every event was conspiring to make me more reckless. For most of the last four years, sex had been the furthest thing from my mind. I'd honestly wondered if I'd ever want to have sex again. I knew precisely what I wanted now, or perhaps I should say who. Alex.

I was still a little grumpy about his whole not rushing thing, but I'd already discovered it didn't take much from me to knock through his manufactured control. I was determined he'd stop worrying about it. I figured he might be the ideal man for what I had in mind—a fling of nothing but sex. It was quite convenient that his presence alone was enough to make me wet and panting. I also trusted him completely, which was saying something.

For a while, I hadn't believed I'd ever trust any man enough with my body. I wasn't so far gone inside that I didn't believe any man could be trusted. I watched Olivia fall in love with Liam and knew beyond a shadow of a doubt he cherished her and was madly in love and lust with her. My parents had a good marriage, and I knew my dad would never hurt my mom. I even had male friends I trusted. Yet, I'd believed I couldn't let down my guard enough to want someone again. I'd thought getting raped had broken something inside me. Ever since that day a few weeks back when I ran into Alex in the park, I'd realized maybe it didn't have to stay that way. I wasn't sure why I hadn't noticed him this way before because he was eye candy and a soccer star to boot, but I hadn't. Although we'd barely spent any time alone together, so maybe it was as simple as that.

Daisy cleared her throat, alerting me to the fact I'd wandered off in my mind. I looked back at her. "That's the plan," I said firmly. Whenever I thought about it, a tiny voice nudged me inside. I wasn't so sure what Alex thought of just a fling. That voice also wasn't so sure this was a good idea for my heart. I didn't care to think about that right now. My body was mine again, and I intended not to miss out on something I'd wondered if I'd ever enjoy again.

Daisy eyed me thoughtfully. "Look, I think it's great you're interested in any guy, okay? I just don't know if a 'nothing but sex' fling is the way to go about this. I'm also not sure what Alex might think of that. Have you talked to him about this?"

Daisy was ever practical when it came to matters like this. She'd been on a self-declared mission to find the love of her life the last year or so and was open to the point of hilarity about it. I'd gently pointed out perhaps she should relax and let life happen, but that wasn't really Daisy's personality. I was slightly taken aback she thought there needed to be advance discussion with Alex.

"I mean, he knows I want him if that's what you mean," I offered with a shrug.

"Well, there's wanting someone and then there's what you're proposing, which is basically using him for sex. He might be all about that, but I don't know. Alex is, well, he's not really a player."

I swallowed the last of my coffee and considered her point. Alex played his cards so close to his chest when it came to personal matters, I didn't have much to go on to suss out what he might think. He eschewed the media attention that came with being an international sports star and had never been linked publicly with anyone that I knew. This was in contrast to some of his teammates from the Seattle Stars and his former team in England. If I listened to what my heart tried to whisper, it made me question myself, so I kept ignoring it. Those whispers said Alex didn't do much lightly. Those whispers made my heart race and anxiety bloom in my chest. Just getting to the point where I could enjoy the feeling of desire again was so huge, it was too much to think beyond that. I didn't want to miss out on this, so I swatted those whispers away.

"Maybe he's not, but I don't see why that should stop me," I finally said.

Daisy's perceptive gaze coasted over me. After a beat, she asked, "Something happen to trigger this?"

Annoyed, I rolled my eyes. "Why can't it just be that maybe I'm finally getting past what happened? You've never said it, but I'm sure you've wondered if I really ever would."

Because she was that kind of friend, Daisy didn't back down and let me derail her. "Hey, I'm thrilled for you. I really am. I never wondered if it made sense that you didn't date. Honestly, it did. I think everyone can find what they want however it works for them. It certainly doesn't mean sex and relationships are the key. If there's one thing I've wanted for you, it's for you to call the shots about this. You seem to be doing that right now. But I've got a feeling there's something behind all this and it's not just how hot Alex is. Trust me, I think the guy's worth drooling over, but he doesn't do a thing for me. I just think…"

I cut her off. "Fine. Maybe something did trigger this, but I think it's a good thing. I saw Joe. Three times actually." I crossed my arms and all but glared at her.

Daisy's eyes flashed, and she leaned her elbows on the table. "You saw Joe Schmidt?"

"Yeah. I did. He must live near the park by my place because I saw him running there twice now and once in his car on the street. Before you go flipping out, there's nothing to do about him existing. I can't keep living my life trying to avoid him. I'm not happy I saw him. At all. But it's weird because seeing him and not falling apart again tells me I'm okay. Maybe that triggered something, but I don't know if it matters. I like Alex, and you just said it yourself—he's worth drooling over, so I might as well enjoy him while I can." My heart kicked up a notch saying this aloud.

Daisy was quiet, her gaze searching my face. For a flash, I recalled the look on her face the day I'd been raped. I'd called her and Olivia from the police station. Olivia hadn't gotten my message until later because she'd been taking an exam. Daisy had raced to the police station after rolling out of bed. She'd stuck to me like glue for weeks afterwards.

Between her and Olivia, I'd barely had a moment alone. She was a loyal, caring and ferociously protective friend. I crossed and uncrossed my legs, restless under her appraisal.

Daisy leaned back in her chair and sighed. "Hon, I'm all for you enjoying whoever you want. Just be careful. Don't hurt yourself in the process. You're not really a fling person."

I chewed on the inside of my cheek and flipped a sugar packet in circles between my fingers. I'd never had a fling in my life. Before the awfulness of getting raped, I'd had a whopping total of two semi-serious relationships, both of which lasted roughly two years. Each had ended in a similar fashion, mostly a slow fade and ending on friendly terms. The more recent of the two, Ross Palmer, had occupied my sophomore and junior years in college. He'd reached out after the whole mess with Joe exploded in the news. He'd been nothing but supportive through it all. If there'd been any chance for a spark to return between us, it would've, yet it hadn't. We still stayed in touch sporadically. He lived in Seattle with his latest girlfriend. I tried to recall if I'd even considered a fling before my life fell apart. I hadn't, so I should probably be wondering what the hell I was thinking. I didn't want to though. I wanted to run at this and tumble into it because I hadn't thought I'd ever experience desire again. Most certainly not the scalding hot desire I felt for Alex.

I looked to Daisy and wondered what I'd been hoping to hear from her. I had wanted to talk, if anything because I had enough sense to know I might need someone to ground me. Daisy wasn't calling me crazy, yet she was planting questions, and I wasn't too thrilled with that. "I'm not the same person I was before. I never will be," I finally said.

Daisy smiled softly, her eyes warm. "Of course not, but even though you're different, there's a part of you that's the same. I'm just not sure that Harper is a fling type. I'd have said you were a nester. I'd say the same about Alex too. He's just got that vibe."

"A nester?"

"Yeah, you nest into relationships and make them cozy." She shrugged and waved a hand. "That's not what you want right now. I'm backing off because you know what? If you want a sex fling with Alex Gordon, who am I to tell you not to go for it? God knows, plenty of women will be jealous. He's got that whole hard-to-get vibe down to a science. Even worse, he's not even trying. It's just the way he is." She grinned and reached over to squeeze my hand. "Just know if you need me, I'm here."

That evening, I almost jumped when my phone buzzed on the table. Stanley was seated at my feet with his giant head resting on one of them. I leaned forward and snagged my phone off the coffee table to see Alex's name on the banner.

Walking to your place now. See you in a bit.

I grinned and then laughed aloud at myself. I was downright giddy over seeing Alex again. Maybe I was crazy, but I didn't particularly care just now. Stanley lifted his head, his solemn blue gaze assessing me. "Okay, Stanley, you had your walk, so now you can nap while I go out to dinner," I informed him.

I didn't care whether or not he knew precisely what I was saying. I talked to him anyway. My father had gotten Stanley for me from a rescue program in the months after Joe raped me. Stanley had been my rock of solace in the loneliest, darkest time of my life. After a moment, he nudged my calf with his nose.

"Oh right!" I jumped up, suddenly realizing if Alex was on his way, I needed to be downstairs to meet him. I grabbed my purse off the table and a jacket by the door. Stanley padded to the door and looked up expectantly. "Be good," I said, quickly leaning over to drop a kiss on the top of his dappled gray head. I knew he'd most likely sleep straight through until morning. Once he'd had his evening walk, that's what he did.

After locking the door behind me, I jogged down the stairs, realizing as I reached the bottom that I hadn't walked anywhere morning or night when it was close to dark in years. I likely wouldn't have now, yet Alex would be with me, so the question of fear didn't even cross my mind. I saw him approaching and walked outside to meet him. Waiting on the bottom step, my pulse kicked up a notch just watching him walk toward me. He was a near perfect specimen of pure masculine strength. He was on the tall side, his form muscled and sleek. His shoulders flexed with the swing of his arms. He stopped in front of me, his eyes level with mine from where I stood a step above the sidewalk.

It was early evening and the sun was setting. The light was smudgy and gray, and the sky streaked with pink in the distance over Puget Sound. Alex looked to me, his brown eyes dark and unfathomable. In a flash, the air around us felt heated. His mere presence made me hot inside and out. That recklessness rose within, and I wanted to grab onto him and drag him upstairs. But I held back. I was bound and determined tonight wouldn't end with him putting the brakes on anything, yet I knew if I was too demanding, he'd hold the line.

"Shall we?"

The low timbre of his voice sent a shiver over my skin. My belly clenched and heat slid through my veins. I couldn't seem to form a word, but I managed a nod and stepped down to the sidewalk. Without a word, we began walking. We were meeting at a restaurant roughly a fifteen minute walk away. I'm not sure who reached for whose hand, but somewhere along the way, I found my hand clasped in Alex's. His hand dwarfed mine—his grip strong and warm as he held my hand lightly. My attention narrowed to that point of contact, savoring it. My mind wandered to what his hands felt like on my skin.

By the time we reached the restaurant and Alex ushered me inside, I was hot and bothered to the point of ridiculous. I wasn't sure what the occasion was, although I'd come to learn Liam liked to eat. A lot. He liked Olivia with him all the time, so he tended to round up friends for no reason other than dinner together. We were meeting at a place I'd never been tonight—an Italian restaurant that was one of the latest new favorites in Seattle. The entryway was crowded. Alex ignored everyone and guided me through with his hand on the curve of my back. He leaned down. "Liam texted they were already here," he said, his gruff voice sending a jolt of need through me.

Goosebumps rose on my skin at the feel of his breath feathering against my neck when he spoke. I had to remind myself we were in public and melting on sight might be embarrassing. I managed to nod and kept walking. Alex winked at the hostess when we reached the small stand where she stood. That's all it took for her to abandon whatever she was doing and smile at him. "What can I do for you?" she asked, actually batting her lashes at him.

"We're meeting a party here. Liam Reed."

I saw the recognition in the hostess's eyes the moment she connected Alex to Liam. They were both well known in and around Seattle since they'd been signed by the aggressive management for the Seattle Stars. Seattle aimed for international attention with their soccer team, and Liam, Alex and their other British teammates were part of that push. "Oh yes, Mr. Gordon. Right this way," she said with a beaming smile.

Her eyes never flicked my way. If Alex was affected in the slightest by her, it didn't show. If anything, he looked more bored while she chattered brightly at him as she led us across the restaurant to a large round table tucked into a corner at the back of the restaurant. Liam and Olivia sat together with Liam's arm thrown across her shoulders as he laughed at something Tristan Wells said. Tristan was the fourth soccer player recruited from Britain. Of them, I'd seen him the least since Olivia had started dating Liam and I'd been brought into the orbit of their world. While Liam and Ethan were the fun-loving flirts, Alex and Tristan were more somber. Tristan had black locks that were almost always rumpled and hazel eyes. As would be expected given most of his life was dedicated to playing soccer at an elite level, he was in incredible condition. I'd gotten to know him a little and learned he was finishing up his coursework for medical school. How he managed that while he played professional sports was beyond me.

Olivia glanced up. "Oh hey! You're both

here. Sit," she said, patting the chair beside her.

I rounded the table and slipped into the seat, suddenly aware that I'd been so zoned out over Alex I forgot we were in public. Alex sat down beside me without a word. This wasn't unusual. In fact, his tendency to be quiet was probably why I hadn't talked to him much before the last few weeks. Liam leaned forward. "Glad you made it, mate," he said with a wink and an easy grin.

Alex smiled slightly. "You knew I'd make it," he replied in greeting.

"Right you are," Liam said with a shrug. His bright blue eyes landed on me. "And the lovely Harper. How are you?"

For the thousandth time, I could do nothing other than laugh at his greeting. Liam was an unabashed flirt. If he wasn't so ridiculously in love with Olivia, someone who didn't know him might wonder. He insisted on calling me lovely, I think, because he knew it bothered me a little. With a roll of my eyes, I replied, "I'm fine, Liam. You?"

"Right as rain," he replied with a wink before turning to Alex again. "Okay mate, bets on how much we'll win our next game by."

Alex shrugged and chuckled softly. "Pass."

Liam rolled his eyes and promptly swung to Tristan. "You were right."

Tristan smiled slightly, but stayed quiet.

"Right about what?" I asked.

Olivia caught my eyes with a smile and a slow shake of her head. "Tristan said Alex wouldn't bother guessing. No one will bet with Liam, so he'll be pestering me next." She paused to take a sip of wine and tuck a loose curl behind her ear.

Liam grinned and reached for the very curl she'd just pushed out of the way. He pulled it out and let it go where it bounced against her cheek. She flushed and rolled her eyes. With her dark curls, ivory skin and green eyes, Olivia was the lovely one. Until Liam, I'd occasionally wondered if she'd ever focus on anything other than work. It was good to see her with Liam. Beyond the fact she actually had a life outside of work now, they were silly happy together. With their dog Bentley, they were their own unit now. My thoughts spun to my earlier conversation with Daisy. I knew why she questioned me and the whole fling idea, but thinking beyond that made me uncomfortable inside. I worried if I started wishing for more, that itself would get in the way.

As if conjured by my thoughts, Daisy

strolled up to the table, stopping at the edge and scanning those of us already seated. "Well, hello then. I suppose I'm late."

Tristan glanced up at her. "You're still not later than Ethan."

Daisy beamed and sat down with flourish beside him. "That's why I like you, Tristan. You're so exacting."

Tristan arched a brow but said nothing more. Within moments, conversation carried on around me. A waiter arrived to take our orders and somewhere in the middle of that, Ethan arrived. Alex and I were seated just where the table was tucked into the corner. It felt almost as if we were in our own bubble with comments bandying back and forth and around us, yet everyone seemed content to let us lay low. We were each respectively the quietest of our clusters of friends. Here and there, I noticed Daisy's gaze flicking to us curiously, but she held back from teasing, which was a miracle, all things considered.

The food was genuinely delicious. Seattle's trendiness was sometimes a problem, or so I thought. New places would spring up and be declared amazing, yet didn't always fit the bill. The food here met my standard for amazing. I drank more wine than I probably should have. With Alex's close presence revving my nerves and adrenaline to high idle, I sought relief in the subtle buzz. I hadn't realized when, but his hand had landed on my thigh under the table. In the midst of Ethan telling a rambling story about a game they won a few weeks ago, I lost focus on everyone around us, my attention zeroed in on Alex and Alex alone. The heat of his touch branded me. His thumb stroked in idle passes just on the inside of my thigh. I was slick with need from nothing other than his subtle touch.

My breath was shallow, and damn me to hell, but I wanted him so badly I was frantic inside. My pulse was running off wildly, and I scrambled to get my body under control. I made the mistake of glancing to him. His hooded gaze met mine, his eyes like dark chocolate. His look was so fierce, I felt a hot throb at the apex of my thighs. I suddenly didn't give a damn what anyone might wonder about us and stood abruptly.

"I need to get home," I blurted out.

Ethan stopped mid-sentence, his teasing gaze perusing over me. "Am I boring you?" he asked in his slightly haughty British accent.

I shook my head sharply. "Not at all. I just have to go. Stanley probably needs a walk," I lied, trying to come up with some reason. All

I knew was I couldn't keep sitting here, or I'd tackle Alex.

I started to push past Alex, but he stood quickly. "I'll walk you home then."

My body sent up a hallelujah.

As I hurried around the table, I caught Daisy's knowing glance and Olivia's curious one, but I ignored them. My body was of two minds—either I'd have Alex, all of him, tonight, or I'd at least tear myself out of this hours long teasing foreplay. I'd never have considered sitting beside someone for dinner foreplay, but with Alex it was.

I walked quickly through the restaurant and pushed through the doors outside. Cool rain hit my heated cheeks, reminding me I'd forgotten to get my jacket. I started to turn back, only to find Alex right behind me. Without a word, he held my jacket for me to slip on. Once it was settled over my shoulders, his palms slid down my arms. I shivered, more from the feel of his touch than anything.

ALEX

I walked beside Harper, fighting an all out war inside my head. My cock had been rock hard and ready for a good hour. Bloody hell. Just sitting beside her had been a torment and a tease all evening. If my body had its way, there would be no more waiting. So there was that, and then my damn it all to hell conscience. I knew it would infuriate Harper, but I couldn't help but wonder what was driving her like this. I also couldn't keep the fact of her rape out of my mind. I didn't know for certain, but I definitely got the sense from Olivia that Harper hadn't dated anyone since it happened, so it wasn't likely she'd had sex either. She didn't strike me as the type to seek out casual encounters, which mucked my brain up even more because I didn't know what she was after with me. Oh, I knew we had chemistry, hell we had enough chemistry to burn down a house. Yet, I didn't know what lay beyond that. I knew for me, Harper wasn't just a way to get my needs met. She was a hell of a lot more than that.

I almost stumbled when she came to an abrupt stop outside my apartment steps. Since my apartment was a few blocks closer to the restaurant than hers, I'd expected to keep walking. She turned and looked up at me. She hadn't bothered with the hood of her jacket, so her hair was damp. The dark locks gleamed under the streetlights. "How's Callie?" she asked.

For a beat, I was puzzled before my brain kicked into gear. I'd forgotten she'd encountered me checking on the little stray calico who'd been camping under the stairs. That had been the last time she'd gone and blown my mind by kissing me. My mind skipped tracks to the feel of her flexing against me as she came all over my fingers. I gave myself a mental kick. *Not now, mate.*

"Callie's still hanging around. Let's see," I stepped to the base of the stairs and looked underneath. Callie's eyes caught the light as she turned my way. She was snuggled into the blanket I'd left there for her. I started to straighten and almost collided with Harper who'd leaned down to look.

"Oh, she's all cozy," Harper said softly.

Harper glanced me to, her face inches away, and it was all I could do not to kiss her. My heart beat a hard rhythm as I looked at her. She reached a hand toward Callie, carefully keeping it far enough away so as not to be threatening. Callie leaned her nose forward and sniffed before shifting back again and eyeing us cautiously. "I wish she'd come in. It's wet and cold out," Harper said softly.

"Aye. You and me both. My landlord's been feeding her too. Between us, I figure she'll eventually decide it's safe to come inside."

I straightened and took a breath. I needed a minute to get some kind of control over my body. In the battle between my mind and body, my body definitely held the upper hand. Harper stood and looked up at me. Drops of rain rolled down her cheeks and before I realized what I was doing, I was wiping a drop away from under her eye. I froze, my eyes locked to hers. Lust hit me like a bolt. Barely holding the gates closed against the rampaging need Harper elicited, it took every ounce of discipline I had not to lift her in my arms and find the closest place to bury myself inside of her.

She held still, her eyes searching mine. Suddenly, she grabbed my hand and spun around, tugging me up the stairs behind her. She tried to open the door to my building, but it was locked, logically so. She spun back, her eyes flashing. "Let me in."

I doubted she meant it that way, but her words held a double meaning. What she didn't know was she was already burrowed so deep inside of me, I was knocked back on my heels. This wasn't a place I was accustomed to. Rather, my years of working to be everything my father wasn't had whetted my discipline and control. Being a goalkeeper day in and day out under the high pressure of the international football world honed qualities of calm, cool, collected and razor sharp attention. Harper rattled me in more ways than one. Right now, all I wanted was her, but I knew she wanted nothing but all of it, and I didn't know if I had the ability to hold back.

She grabbed my shirt, fisting it in her hand, and yanked me to her. Her head banged against the door behind her, and I reflexively reached to catch her. Between her tugging me toward her and me reaching for her, her lips were suddenly within a whisper of mine. My body went taut, every fiber flexing toward her, unable to resist the surge of lust.

I dragged a breath in and thought for a second I'd latched onto a thread of control. She tightened her grip on my shirt and locked her eyes with mine. It felt as if a match lit the air between us. With cool drizzle falling all around us, the air felt electric. I couldn't think over the drumming of my heart and the blood shooting straight to my groin. I yanked my keys out of my pocket and reached around her to open the door. She stumbled back when it gave way. I did what I'd wanted to do for weeks and lifted her into my arms. I meant to bundle her against me, but she was having none of that. Her legs curled around my hips. In the jumble, her lips crashed to mine and my control, frayed beyond all reason, snapped. I held her tight against me and kicked the door shut behind me.

With every step I took, Harper's tongue warred with mine. She kissed with wild abandon. Considering I was nearly on fire inside, it was a tangle of lips, teeth and tongue. I shouldered through the door into my flat, tearing my lips free from hers to groan when she rocked her hips against me. By some small miracle, I didn't stumble and fall getting to the bedroom and managed to turn and sit down. She was still tangled around me and shoved my jacket off my shoulders. Her hips sank down on me, and bloody hell, it felt so fucking good to feel the heat of her against me. I shook my arms free from my jacket and tossed it aside before gripping her hips and holding her down, arching into her. My cock was so hard it ached, and all I could think about was the sweet slick heat I knew awaited me.

She cried out, her eyes whipping open. Dark blue gaze flashing, her lips parted on a low moan when I flexed into the cradle of her hips. She stared at me and for a flash I saw the wheels start turning in her brain. I did the opposite of what I'd have expected had I been in a rational state of mind. In that scenario, I'd have thought perhaps we shouldn't rush through this. Not with the weight of her past in the room with us. Yet now, with the air nearly vibrating with the force of desire between us, all I knew was if there was only one thing I could give her, it would be to tumble headlong into this wild pulse of longing, lust and then some between us.

I eased my grip on her hips and pushed

her jacket off her shoulders, sliding my palm up her spine to thread my hand in her hair. "Don't start thinking on me, Harper. That's not what this is about," I whispered fiercely just before slamming my mouth to hers again and pouring everything I felt into our kiss.

I lost all sense of time. A tangled jumble of clothes being torn off in the midst of hot kisses, Harper's hands roving everywhere and pushing me to the edge of sanity. I clung to the thinnest thread, determined to make sure she found the pinnacle of pleasure before this was over. Trust me, it wasn't easy. I liked sex just about any way—soft and slow, fast and hard, rough and wild. Harper hit me so hard, I wanted to pound into her, desperate for release. Yet, I didn't want to push her too far. Bloody hell, she didn't make it easy. She was all over me, her hands everywhere while she kissed, licked and nipped at me.

Somehow, I untangled myself and stood. Our clothes were strewn in a messy montage on the bed and floor. Harper rested on her elbows and looked up at me. Damn, she was gorgeous. She had an athletic build, softened only by her lush curves. Her breasts were damp from where I'd mapped my way over them with my mouth, her nipples taut and deep pink.

Her breath came in short pants, and her eyes locked to me. "What...?"

I ignored her and leaned over to hook my hands under her knees, tugging her roughly to the end of the bed. Without waiting to see how she might react, I pushed her knees apart. She was so wet, her folds slick with her need. I dragged a finger through them, but didn't wait anymore and brought my mouth against her. She tensed for a flash, and I wondered if I'd taken this the wrong direction. Then, she moaned and her knees relaxed when her hands threaded into my hair. I settled in to taste her and drive her mad. My only goal: nothing but pure pleasure for her.

I slid a finger into her channel as I explored her with my tongue. Another finger joined the first, and I savored the feel of her clenching around me and her hips bucking against my mouth. Far faster than I expected, I could feel her quickening and she cried out, her hands tightening their grip on my hair as she pulsed around my fingers. I slowly eased away. As I stood and leaned across the bed to snatch a condom out of the nightstand, I experienced a flash of concern. Harper was no virgin and certainly didn't act like a woman who needed to be handled with care. But hell. She'd been raped and as far as I knew, this might be the first time she'd had sex since then.

I looked down at her and promptly forgot that train of thought. She was leaning up on her elbows, watching and waiting. Her skin glistened in the dim light filtering from the living room, her hair was a rumpled mess and her eyes were dark. I rolled the condom on and stretched out over her. Holy hell. It felt so good to feel her against me. Her skin was damp, her sweat mingling with mine. She was a mix of soft and firm, her muscles flexing as she curled her legs around my hips. I told myself I should go slow, but what I said in my head and how my body responded to her were two entirely different things. When I felt her slick heat against my cock, I was gone.

I brushed her tangled hair away from her face. I needed to look at her. "Harper."

Her eyes flew open, and I traced her brows with a fingertip. My heart was pounding so hard, it reverberated through my body. Her breath came in soft gusts. She tightened her legs and arched into me. "Alex, don't make me wait."

Her rough whisper was like an arrow. Straight to the heart—its hit almost painful. My body answered her, arching and sinking into her wet, velvet clench. Her eyes fell closed and her breath came out in a low moan, while I forced myself to hold still. She was tight. Whether she was aware or not, she tensed. After a few beats, I could feel her easing around me.

Chapter Ten

HARPER

Finally.

I sighed and bit back another moan. Alex felt so good—all of him, inside me and against me. I was tight, tighter than I'd have imagined, and he was, well, no one would ever claim he wasn't well-endowed. I hadn't meant to tense, but I did. Out of reflex, or something else. After a minute, it passed, and I relaxed. He was all muscle and sensual power surrounding me. I could feel him nearly vibrating against me and sensed him holding back. I slid a palm down his back, savoring every muscled inch of it and arched into him. If he meant to be gentle, I wasn't having it.

"Alex," I whispered fiercely.

His head had fallen into the dip of my neck, and he lifted it. His dark brown gaze met mine. I could see the immense control he was exerting, and I wanted him to stop. "Don't."

"Don't what?"

"Hold back."

"Harper..."

I spurred my heels and flexed against him, unable to hide the rush of satisfaction when he reflexively arched into me.

He moved swiftly, gripping my hands in his and stretching them above my head. I wanted hard, fast and rough—something I could lose myself in. He didn't give me that. He settled into a rhythm—maddeningly slow, yet every stroke just deep enough he drove me higher and higher inside.

I lost myself, but not in the way I'd imagined. I tumbled into a slow, hot dance of longing and need, the pressure building inside so intensely, I thought I might explode. Every stroke of him filling me, the slow pull and drag in my channel spun me tighter and tighter. All the while, his eyes were on me, his hands gripping mine, and I felt vulnerable, raw and exposed. Because I trusted him completely, so completely it almost frightened me. He eased his grip and dragged his hand down between us. A flick of his thumb against my clit and pleasure spun loose, whipping through me in a rush.

One more deep stroke and he went rigid against me before a guttural cry broke loose. His head fell into my shoulder again, and he immediately eased his weight to one side.

We lay still, our breath coming in heaves. After a few moments, my pulse slowed enough I could think. Reality started to sink in. I was warring inside—torn between wanting to dance with joy because I'd finally had sex and a reflexive need to withdraw from the depth of intimacy I felt with Alex. My brain turned on, rarely a good sign, and I opened my eyes to find Alex's warm brown gaze waiting.

I suddenly worried he'd want to talk, but he didn't say a word. He simply brushed my tangled hair off my forehead. Okay. That felt good. I could do this.

Hours later, I woke in the darkness. For a moment, I was disoriented and muddled panic rose inside. I started to roll over when my consciousness flickered enough to remind me the warm body beside me was Alex. He was spooned behind me, his breathing even and steady. Even in sleep, his body felt strong. His muscled arm was hooked over my hip, his palm resting on my belly. I lay still and took a slow breath, feeling silly at my initial panic.

I'd had nightmares off and on for years after Joe raped me. At first, they'd visited me almost nightly. My doctor had gently suggested I try something to help me sleep after seeing me ragged and weary after too many nights of bad sleep. When I'd refused, she'd handed me a card for a therapist. After weeks of fighting against myself, I'd gone to see the therapist mostly out of desperation because trying to live without sleep was nearly impossible when it went on too long. It was like being kicked into a ditch every night, each day afterwards a slow crawl out. With some help, I'd managed to get a handle on my sleep and on my panic attacks. Those old nightmares rarely visited me anymore, and I hadn't had an actual panic attack in almost two years. I supposed waking in the night with a man beside me for the first time in over four years might be disconcerting.

I hadn't thought past what my body had been craving for the last few weeks. Finally breaking through a barrier I'd worried might exist for the rest of my life and actually having sex was such an immense relief. I'd known the chemistry with Alex was bordering on singe-worthy. Yet, I couldn't have known he'd proceed to drive me mad with pleasure. I couldn't have known the intimacy that would bind me to him and the intense vulnerability I'd feel. My mind spun to Daisy's observation that I wasn't a fling type, but a nester. A flash of panic rose within, an entirely different kind of panic. What the hell had I done?

I started to carefully move away from Alex, but my subtle motion nudged him out of sleep. His hand slid across my belly and sloped over the curve of my hip in a lazy caress. The calloused skin of his palm sent a shiver through me.

I couldn't have moved away if my life depended on it now. It felt too good to be there. He murmured in my hair. I rolled my head. "Hm?"

His eyes opened. There was a glimmer of light cast by a nightlight by his bed. In that tiny bit of light, his eyes caught mine. His palm stroked along my side and down again. "Go back to sleep," he murmured.

Instead of my mind spinning its wheels, I fell asleep—too relaxed, too warm and feeling too safe to do anything else.

———

That afternoon, I settled in to clean like crazy. What better time to clean like a mad-woman than after my world had been knocked on its axis—in a frighteningly good way—by one night with Alex? I scrubbed the kitchen spotless and vacuumed my entire apartment. Stanley laid down for a nap with an aggrieved sigh after dodging the vacuum a few too many times. My mind had been spin-ning its wheels ever since I'd closed the door behind Alex after he walked me home early this morning. He'd offered to walk with me when I took Stanley out, but I'd declined. Usually we'd be running, but the morning was, well, weird for me. I'd needed some way to create some space for myself. In part be-cause I'd so desperately wanted to latch my-self to Alex and be with him all the time.

Aside from the enormity of finally—fi-nally!—having sex again, I felt like flotsam in the rough seas of my emotions. Elation, de-sire, anger, sadness, longing and, above all, confusion rolled through me in wave after wave. Last night with Alex had been so far beyond anything I'd expected, I couldn't even compute what to do about it. All I'd wanted was to experience the deep desire I felt for him. I couldn't have anticipated it would be so much more than simply that. I'd gotten everything I could have ever hoped for in terms of the whole sex part of it. For so long, I'd worried I'd never even manage to get through the act itself that I'd figured it would be luck if I felt desire and had sex without incidence.

Alex had blown the hinges off any doors on my expectations. Hell, I couldn't recall sex even coming close to what we'd had...ever. On the level of the physical experience, it was out of this world. Then there was the emotional part. That's what had me rocking in the waves inside. I wasn't prepared to feel as if the shadow cast over my heart had dissipated into nothing under the blinding brightness of how it felt to be with him. I felt as if my heart had tripped and landed on its ass this morning, knocked down by the force of so much unexpected emotion. I was scared shitless and needed time to regroup.

I was in the midst of cleaning the bathroom when my doorbell rang. I initially ignored it. Then it rang two more times, rather insistently. I tossed the sponge in the tub and rinsed my hands before walking to answer the door. Opening it, I found Daisy and Olivia there.

Daisy held a bag of pastries aloft and swept past me. "We're here for brunch," she announced as she aimed straight for the kitchen.

Olivia held up two cups of coffee from Desert Isle Café, handing me one. "Hi," she said with a soft grin. "Daisy insisted we drop in. Hope it's okay."

I waved her inside. "Come on in." I knew Daisy was there to get the scoop on Alex. I could seriously use some girl-talk, but I felt odd, almost as if talking about what happened with Alex wasn't right. It had been so intimate, I was so shaken I didn't know what to do, or to even ask.

Daisy promptly started opening cabinets until she found the plates. I'd only moved in here a few months ago, so she wasn't familiar with what went where. We tended to treat each other's apartments as if we lived there. Olivia plunked down on the couch and patted the spot beside her. "Come sit. Let's enjoy our coffee while Daisy waits on us," she said with a wink.

"Please do," Daisy called with a laugh.

I settled on the couch beside Olivia, tucking a foot under me and taking a welcome sip of coffee. Seconds later, Daisy walked over, balancing two plates on one arm with her coffee and another plate barely balanced in the other. I reached up and took a tipsy plate off her forearm. "You could've asked for help."

"I like a challenge," she said as she set the remaining plates on the coffee table and sat down on the other side of the sectional.

I took a bite of a flaky spinach and cheese roll. "So good," I managed after another bite. I glanced between them. "So what's up?"

Daisy's round brown eyes scanned my face. "Okay, what's wrong?"

Sometimes I hated how hard it was to hide my feelings. I wasn't too good at acting like everything was fine when it wasn't.

I glanced to Olivia, as if she might rescue me from Daisy's directness. All I found in her eyes was searching concern.

"Nothing," I finally replied, trying and failing to keep the hint of defensiveness out of my tone.

Daisy didn't say a word and simply took a sip of coffee.

Olivia cleared her throat, and I thought for a beat she might save me from this conversation. Then she spoke. "*Are* you okay?"

Fighting the flush on my cheeks, I sighed. "Of course I'm okay! Why wouldn't I be? What is it with this anyway?"

Daisy lasered me with her direct and way too perceptive gaze. "Cut the shit. As far as we could see, you were about to climb in Alex's lap and screw his brains out last night. Which is fine with me, by the way. But you look pretty damn upset right now. That's not fine with me."

Emotion knotted my throat and tears pushed at the backs of my eyes. I took a breath and a gulp of coffee. "Do I look that bad?" I asked, glancing between them.

Daisy nodded emphatically, while Olivia was quiet. After a moment, she shrugged. "I wouldn't say you look bad, but you look... stressed," she finally said.

I took another gulp of coffee, savoring its bitterness. "I guess I am. Um," I paused and looked to Daisy. "Did you..?"

"Tell her about your crazy idea to have a sex fling with Alex? I kinda had to after last night. It was pretty damn obvious. I thought you two were going to burst into flames on sight."

I sighed and leaned back into the cushions. Looking between them, I flushed. "I didn't realize we were that obvious."

"Oh, you were," Daisy said with a sharp laugh. "It was almost funny, but now I'm worried about what happened."

When I looked to Olivia, her eyes narrowed. "Are you okay?" she asked, circling back to Daisy's earlier question.

Realizing they were starting to head in the worst possible direction about why I might be stressed, I figured I'd better nip that in the bud. "I might be stressed, but don't start thinking it's because I tried to have sex and fell apart."

"Okaaay... Care to explain?" Daisy asked slowly.

"We had sex, and it was amazing," I replied, almost angrily. I wasn't angry at Daisy for being this pushy. I knew if I'd been the friend of someone in my situation, I'd probably have worried. Daisy was, of course, naturally nosy and didn't care to hide it, but she didn't feel nosy now. Just concerned.

Daisy cocked her head to the side. "Amazing?"

"Uh huh. And that's the whole problem."

Olivia eyed me. "Why is that a problem?"

"Because...because it wasn't supposed to be like this!"

"What was it supposed to be like?" Olivia asked.

I threw a hand up, letting it fall to the couch with a thump. "I just wanted to, well, to have sex. I didn't want any complications. Just something neat and tidy."

Daisy, remarkably, stayed quiet. She'd warned me of this very issue when she shared her concern I wasn't a fling type of person.

When Olivia spoke, her tone was cautious. "When did you start hunting around for sex? Last I knew, you'd sworn off relationships." She paused for a sip of coffee, angling her head to the side. "Don't get me wrong, I didn't think it was the best idea to permanently put yourself on the sidelines, and Alex is awesome, but..."

Her words ran out, and I knew she was trying to avoid bumping into the topic that was always the elephant in the room when it came to discussing me and anything to do with sex and relationships. An incredibly annoying side effect of getting raped was how everyone tiptoed around certain topics. I took a gulp of coffee and looked back at Olivia. "How many times have I said I'm sick of people tiptoeing around the obvious? I'll say it for you. You didn't think it was a great idea for me to avoid men for the rest of my life just because some guy raped me."

Olivia's breath drew in sharply, and she looked hurt. I glanced to Daisy who was quiet, but her face held a studied calm, as if she was doing her damnedest not to let anything show on her face. I suddenly felt horrible. I shook my head sharply. "I'm sorry. I know it's weird. I just get tired of how weird it is."

Olivia tilted sideways on the couch and hugged me hard before leaning back. "Don't be sorry. You have nothing to be sorry for. It's weird and awful, and I wish I could make it all go away."

I swallowed against the emotion rising inside and nodded. "Me too." In an endeavor to get the conversation onto lighter territory, I continued, "You, of all people, should understand the idea of not wanting to bother with relationships. Your only excuse was working too much."

Olivia laughed softly. "True."

"Yeah, that lasted about five minutes when she met Liam," Daisy said with a sly grin.

"It was more than five minutes," Olivia protested, her cheeks turning pink.

"Uh, not to be too hard on you, but didn't you say he kissed you the first time he met you in your office?" I asked.

Olivia rolled her eyes and sighed. "Okay, fine. Maybe so. Anyway, back to you...and Alex. What's wrong with amazing?"

My mind spun back to last night—the feel of Alex's hard body against mine, the delicious stretch of him inside of me and then waking in the darkness in his arms. Probably not what Olivia meant with her question. It occurred to me I was looking for anything to get my mind off of how discombobulated I was inside about everything to do with last night.

I chewed on the inside of my cheek and glanced between them. "Nothing's wrong with amazing. I couldn't have asked for anything better. I just... I don't know if I can do this."

"Do what?" Daisy asked.

I sighed. "The whole emotional messiness. I didn't think about that part."

Daisy, being the fabulous friend she was, didn't even point out that she'd told me so when she had. She scrunched up her nose and sighed heavily. "Right. That part. I wish I knew what to tell you, but I can't even find a guy who makes me feel emotionally messy, so I'm not so much help." She glanced to Olivia. "Your turn."

Olivia didn't miss a beat. "Okay then. Well, it's obvious Alex is totally into you. Maybe you shouldn't worry so much just yet. I mean, you had one night, and no matter who it was, it would have been a thing." She paused and reached for her pastry. After a few bites, she turned back to me, her gaze considering. "I don't know if I should tell you this, but I accidentally said something that led me into telling Alex about what happened to you."

"It's okay. I figured it out."

"Huh?"

If I'd wanted to keep it quiet that I'd seen Joe, that was turning out to be impossible. I barreled ahead. "We saw Joe when we were out running. More than once actually. All I had to do was look at Alex's face and I knew he knew who Joe was. I got a little pissed about it, but he said you told him and he looked Joe up."

Daisy's voice cut in. "She told me about Joe just yesterday. I'm freaking out about it," she said, addressing Olivia.

Olivia finished chewing a bite of her pastry and glanced between us. "I can't keep up. I don't know whether I should be losing my mind over knowing Joe Schmidt is any-where near you, or worried about whatever's going on with Alex." Her eyes coasted over me, concern radiating in her green gaze. "Promise me you'll tell us if you run into Joe again."

"Of course. I didn't want you to worry, so I didn't say anything. I've only seen him in the park and both times Alex was with me."

Olivia's mouth twisted in a sad smile. "And to think I was happy you were running with Alex."

"That's a good thing," I said firmly. "It really is. Honestly, it sucks to see Joe, but I think that's been good too. If anything, seeing him made me realize how much I was letting myself get hobbled by what happened."

Looking between Olivia and Daisy, I saw nothing but concern in their eyes. It was awesome to have friends, especially friends who I knew would do anything for me. But I hated that their concern was all because I'd seen Joe from a distance twice. I couldn't erase what happened, but I could try to move on.

"Could we not get stuck on the whole Joe thing? I'm trying really hard not to do that," I said, taking another bite of my spinach roll.

Daisy nodded so emphatically, her ponytail bounced wildly. "We're not stuck on Joe, Right, Olivia?"

"Of course not. Whatever you want to talk about," she replied.

"Well, I'd say Alex, but I'm not so sure that's a good idea," Daisy said with another scrunch of her nose.

My cheeks got hot and I sighed. "Look, I'm just confused. I don't know what to do now."

Olivia glanced from Daisy to me. I knew she must have talked to Liam about it.

"Okay, what?" I asked

"What, what?" Olivia countered.

Daisy jumped in. "Oh God. Olivia, it's not like she can't figure out you might've talked to Liam. Spill it."

I couldn't help but giggle. As confused as I was, Daisy's directness was funny. At least when it wasn't pointing at me.

Olivia cocked her head to the side and set her now empty plate on the coffee table. "Liam thinks Alex likes you. A lot. He's not a player and pretty much ignores all the women who hang around the team."

My heart gave a hard kick and a funny feeling tightened my chest. My next question popped out before I had a chance to think. "Why does he think Alex likes me?"

"I knew it!" Daisy exclaimed. "You were trying so hard to act like it was just about sex, but you really like him. That's why you're upset." She started to say something else, but snapped her mouth shut.

I could barely focus on Daisy's comment. All I wanted was for Olivia to say more.

My heart gave another kick, and I felt my cheeks heat again. I wasn't quite ready to examine how I felt about Alex, so I shrugged and looked back at Olivia, impatient for her to answer.

"I don't know why. Liam just mentioned it after Alex was over last week. He said if Alex ever fell for anyone, he'd fall hard," Olivia offered. "If you ask me, Alex is a total softie. He's all tough and dark on the outside, but he's so nice. He was like a parent with Liam when he was recovering from his surgery last year, always making sure Liam got to all his appointments. He's a good guy."

"Well, if the way he looked at you last night is any indication, the man is seriously into you. Just sayin.' If he was my cup of tea, I'd have melted on sight," Daisy said with a sigh.

I couldn't help but laugh. I hadn't straightened out much of anything in my own head, but somehow Daisy's comment cast just enough sun inside I managed to find a brief respite from my worries.

Chapter Eleven

ALEX

I strolled down the hallway at the stadium, idly tossing a soccer ball on my way to the locker room. We were done with practice for the day and I was the good kind of tired, physically worn, but floating on the rush of adrenaline from a few hours of play. I rounded the corner in the hall to find Liam leaning against the wall. The moment he saw me, he ended whatever phone call he'd been having. The little snippet of "Bye luv" I heard told me it was Olivia. He flashed a grin. "Good play, mate. Say, are we ready for the game against LA?" he asked as he rested a foot against the wall, clearly expecting me to stop and chat.

"Aye. Think so. You?" I returned as I

leaned against the wall beside him, rolling the ball between my hands.

"Always." He was quiet for a beat before I felt him look my way. "So? Harper," was all he said.

I inwardly groaned. Liam was my best mate and had been for pretty much forever. Yet, he'd always tended toward being more open about his personal life than I was. I didn't mind it so much, but at times like this, it was annoying. I hadn't sorted my own feelings about Harper and here he was asking questions.

I rolled my head to the side on the wall. "What about Harper?"

He rolled his eyes, cracking another sly grin. "Mate, can't believe I'm saying this, but Olivia bossed me into talking to you. I told her you like to keep your private life private, but she's all in a tizzy about whatever the hell is going on with you and Harper. I already swore up and down, left and right that you'd never hurt a woman, but she says I have to talk to you."

My heart gave a hard thump, and I swallowed against the emotion knotting my chest. I rolled my head away from Liam and stared at the wall across from us, my eyes idly following the pattern of tiles on the wall.

Harper. It had been a full two days since my night with her, and I hadn't been able to stop thinking about her. It had been pure heaven to wake up with her lush body curled up against mine. Problem was, once we weren't tangled up together, she'd gone all polite and guarded again. I hadn't wanted to push too hard and comment on it because, hell, if there was a playbook on what to do after you have sex with someone who was raped once upon a time, I didn't have it. So I'd let her be her quiet, reserved self and held back from yanking her back into bed.

We'd gone for our usual run the morning after I woke beside her and again the mornings to follow. I didn't much like thinking about it, but a bit of me was hurt at her polite reserve. Meanwhile, I was wrestling against a need only she could assuage. I'd fought the urge to toss her over my shoulder and cart her upstairs after our run this morning, yet she'd been on the way to work, so I'd held back. The only time I wasn't thinking about her was when I was playing ball. The mental escape that saved my sanity from the ugliness of my father when I was a lad still had the power to keep me focused. Thinking about Harper wasn't something I actually wanted to escape from, yet I was scrambling for a foothold in my mind and heart and body when it came to her. I'd known she wasn't a convenient arrangement, yet I wasn't prepared for how it would feel to be with her.

I rolled my head back toward Liam. "Of course I'd never hurt her. What's Olivia so worried about?"

"Mate, you know what she told you about Harper. Don't play dumb. She says you're the first guy Harper's been interested in since all that went down. She didn't say much about what Harper might think, but she wouldn't shut up about Harper not being a fling kind of person and all that." He paused, his eyes narrowing. "I told her you're not either, so what *is* your deal here?"

Liam played the teasing, superficial role so well, it was easy to forget he was damn perceptive. He might've been happier than me to enjoy the easy pleasures of casual relationships before he found Olivia, but he was a family lad through and through. Once I saw how much Olivia meant to him, I hadn't been surprised in the slightest he fell so hard. He was downright domestic now and loved every minute of it. He also knew me quite well.

I eyed the ball in my hands, bouncing it lightly back and forth. "Harper's no fling for me," I finally said.

"Ah. Right then. I told Olivia that was probably the case. You don't do messy, and it would be a right mess if she was a fling, what with her being one of Olivia's besties. So, I'm not bloody stupid here, but it doesn't sound like you've talked with Harper about how you feel."

Leave it to Liam to hone in right to the point of contention in my own mind. I glanced back to him and rolled my eyes. "Mate, we had one night. It's not like I can see too far ahead."

"Aye. But you're you. I always said you'd fall first, but then I went and beat you to it."

Just as I was pondering how to respond, Coach rounded the corner in the hallway. I breathed a silent sigh of relief. I wasn't up for much more talking about Harper. Not when I was so stirred up in my own head.

Coach paused in front of us. "Hey guys. A heads up we're scheduled for interviews for that bit for the LA sports channel next month."

I bit back a groan. There was one thing I detested about playing football professionally, and it was the media circus. I knew it couldn't be avoided and truth be told, it was better here in the US than back in Britain. There football was close to a religion. Here in the US, their version of football came close, but not soccer. Downside to that was the Seattle Stars management, along with that of the entire US league, was focused on raising the sport's profile here. While it didn't have the fervor of playing in Britain, we were often scheduled for profiles, interviews and the like. I nodded to Coach. "Got it."

Liam chuckled and clapped me on the shoulder as he pushed away from the wall. "You know Alex can't wait," he said, flashing Coach a grin.

Coach's eyes twinkled. "Figured you'd want to know. See you boys tomorrow for practice." He resumed his walk down the hall, turning into his office.

I walked alongside Liam to the locker room, Harper back on the brain.

———

Later that afternoon, I walked down the docks at the harbor, Liam strolling at my side. One thing that hadn't changed since he moved in with Olivia was we still took walks by the harbor after grabbing lunch nearby. We'd developed this habit when we'd been sharing a flat. We'd stop for lunch after practice and meander along the docks for a bit before heading home. Today was breezy and overcast. Gulls called and swooped about in the air. The hum of activity on the docks carried on around us.

No surprise, but I was thinking about Harper. I'd been contemplating how to see her outside of our morning runs. The other night had landed us together by virtue of our mutual friends. I wasn't such a coward I couldn't simply ask her, yet I sensed she might be in a different place than I was when it came to us. With the weight of her past heavy in my mind, I didn't want to push too far too fast. For a flash, I fervently wished I were a different man. My former relationships of pure convenience—tidy and almost business-like—had been so much simpler than this. There was that, and I wasn't one for flings, never had been. I sensed Harper had set out for one thing with me, but I'd be damned if I let it play out that way. As such, I had to play my hand carefully to win her heart the way I wanted.

We reached the top of the docks and headed back toward my flat. Liam would keep going another few blocks to the flat he shared with Olivia. As we turned onto the street that would cross mine, I happened to glance up and see Joe Schmidt. The second I saw him, one thought drove me as I picked up speed—bashing his face in.

I distantly heard Liam call my name, but I'd started running and didn't stop until I reached Joe. He had his keys out and looked as if he was about to get in the car beside him, a nondescript gray sedan. My brain scanned the car and him, filing away the details, so I'd know every time I saw his car. The man who'd shattered Harper's life for a time stood before me. My breath came in deep heaves because I'd sprinted to reach him. At a glance, I knew him for what he was —a mean coward. He had dull blonde hair and light blue eyes. My fury was barely in check, but I clung to the smallest bit of control. He needed to know why I was here.

"Excuse me?" he asked, his gaze confused.

"Alex!" Liam called, his voice closer.

I ignored Liam and stared back at Joe. His gaze cleared and he nodded. "Oh, I know you. I've seen you running at the park with an old friend of mine. Aren't you the goalie for the Seattle Stars?"

What little control I had snapped. "Friend? Do you usually call a woman you raped your friend?" I snarled right before plowing my fist into his face.

Joe's head snapped back with the force of my punch. Blood dripped from his nose, and he sneered at me. "Fuck you."

Liam reached us and grabbed at my arm, but I shook him off and drove my fist in Joe's face again. "That's for Harper."

I'd hit Joe hard enough this time, he fell against the car and stumbled to the ground. I saw nothing but red and started to lean forward and keep at it, but Liam got a good hold on me this go 'round and held firm.

"Mate, ease up. Police are on the way right now," he said, his voice barely filtering through my rage.

I glanced around and the reality of where we were sunk in. We were in a busy section of Seattle by the harbor. Every person nearby was staring at the spectacle I'd created. Joe's face was bloodied and swelling as I looked back at him. Bloody hell.

———

A few hours later I sat across from Coach in his office, staring down at my bruised knuckles. Joe had happily pressed charges against me for assault. Liam had stayed with me through the mess and marched me down to the stadium afterwards, declaring I might as well face the music sooner rather than later. It was a definite possibility I could face a conference penalty for getting charged with assault, not to mention the potential negative publicity for the team. I didn't give a bloody damn, but I knew Liam had a point, so I went along with him.

Coach had met with us together and then asked Liam to wait outside. His countenance was somber and concerned. He watched me quietly before picking up a slinky on his desk and rolling it in a wave between his hands.

"This Harper must mean something to you," he said, his words falling into the heavy quiet.

"Aye. She does. But I'd have punched the guy if he'd raped anyone I knew. Hell, I guess I think all rapists should get their faces bashed in. It's bloody horrible and about the worst thing you can do short of killing someone." My anger had cooled, but I meant my words. It wasn't that I'd spent a hell of a lot of time contemplating how hellish rape was, but it didn't take much to think about. It was the worst sort of crime—a crime of cowardice, one that struck intimately in an ugly way and left scars of pain for the victims.

"Don't disagree with you there. It's just now we've got a bit of a problem to manage.

I can handle the media, but you might have a mess to clean up with Harper. She know what happened yet?"

I shrugged. "No idea. Haven't exactly had a chance to talk to her about it." I'd been busy getting booked for assault charges instead. Even though I didn't regret bashing Joe's face in, I was worried about how Harper might feel about it. The last thing she needed was any publicity about it. There was no way around that though. I cursed myself for not having enough sense to think past the moment.

I took a breath and looked back at Coach. "Any way we can try to ask the media to leave out any revisiting of what happened to Harper?"

Coach sighed and set the slinky down. "We can try, but I looked the guy up as soon as Liam called me from the police station. First online search brings up an article about how he got kicked off the university track team after he was charged for rape. No matter how respectful the journalists want to be, this is a good story. Alex Gordon, soccer star, avenging a woman. I can see it now. I'll do what I can, but it is what it is," Coach said with a slow shake of his head.

Bloody hell. I'd gone and made a mess of

this for Harper. I nodded. "Right then. Am I facing any discipline with the team?"

Coach leaned back in his chair and angled his head to the side. He was quiet so long, I didn't know what to expect. "No. I might have to answer for it, but no. What you did was stupid, but you've owned up to it and, as far as I'm concerned, you had cause. Hell, athletes face no discipline for far worse offenses. We'll have to see if the league thinks otherwise, but we can deal with it. I'll take the heat if I'm defending a guy who punched the man who raped his girlfriend. Go home and cool off."

I met Liam outside Coach's office minutes later. Liam, being the good mate he was, didn't say a word on the way to dropping me off at my flat. I stood outside my place and leaned down to check on Callie. She wasn't there. No surprise given it was midday. I straightened and started walking to Harper's. I needed to see her. Now.

Chapter Twelve

HARPER

At the sound of a knock on my door, I crossed the living room to answer, wondering who it was. Usually Daisy or Olivia would be the only people to stop by unannounced. I swung it open to find Alex standing there. My heart jumpstarted at the sight of him. He had both hands resting on the edges of the doorframe with his head bowed when I opened the door. His brown hair was mussed. He lifted his head, his dark chocolate gaze slamming into mine, and my heart kicked up another notch. His gaze was direct and intense, simmering with feeling.

"Can I come in?" he asked gruffly.

My eyes absorbed the sight of him greedily. I'd barely been able to put the brakes on my thoughts of him ever since the other night. Two days of fevered fantasies and replays of what it felt like to have his hands and mouth mapping my body and the feel of him inside of me when I came. He wore a gray t-shirt that caressed his muscled chest and faded jeans that hugged his legs. I knew what every inch of him felt like underneath. Raw need clawed at me, and I tried to rein my body in. It was no use—having Alex anywhere near me sent my pulse into the stratosphere and heat roaring through me. I managed to nod and step back from the door.

He followed me inside and slipped his hands into his pockets. As I looked at him, I realized he seemed, well, nervous was the only word I could conjure to describe what I sensed. I chewed on my bottom lip, uncertain what to say. "Do you want something to drink? Or eat?" I asked inanely.

He shook his head. After a moment, he rolled his shoulders. "I fucked up," he said suddenly.

"Huh?"

"I saw Joe, and I hit him. Twice," he said flatly.

My stomach churned as I stared back at Alex. I'd like to think I was a better person, one who could rise above the need to punch back at someone who'd hurt me terribly. But I wasn't and I didn't really care just now. A rush of satisfaction rose inside, and my heart felt like it was going to explode.

"You hit him?"

Alex nodded, his gaze worried. "Left him with a bloody nose and a black eye. I'd like to say I regret it, but I don't. Problem is, I got charged with assault and it happened in the middle of a bunch of people. Liam managed to keep me from making more of a spectacle, but I thought you should know because, well because it'll probably end up on the news somewhere."

I heard Alex's words and knew them to be true, but I was so focused on the fact that he'd gone after Joe for me that I didn't really care. "I...I can't believe it. Are you okay? Did he hit you?"

Alex looked so startled, I almost laughed. I doubted it ever occurred to Alex he might not be able to hold his own against Joe, or any man for that matter.

"Of course I'm okay," he finally said. "The only bad part is the charges and the fact there's no way this will stay quiet. I don't care about it for me, but I didn't want it to end up dredging up what happened to you."

I tried to wrap my brain around that, but I simply didn't care. Not right now. "I don't want to think about that," I said, reaching for his hands and giving a little tug.

His hands slid out of his pockets and curled around mine. I took a few steps back until my knees bumped the couch where I sat down. He followed along, sitting down beside me. I didn't quite know what to say, so I repeated my earlier question. "Are you sure you don't want something to drink? I've got coffee ready."

His gaze searched mine before he finally nodded. "Sure."

I bounced up and hurried into the kitchen, snagging two cups from the cabinet and pouring coffee. Within moments, I returned to the couch and handed him a cup. He took a long swallow and sighed before leaning back into the couch. I tucked a foot under my knee as I sat down and curled my hands tightly around my coffee. I tried to plumb the depths of my feelings, but they were a muddle.

In the initial months after Joe raped me, I'd have probably sold my soul to have someone punch him. The need to strike back had been so intense, yet it had been blunted by the mingled feelings of shame and emotional devastation. I learned the hard way it doesn't really matter what people tell you after you get raped. *It's not your fault. There's nothing to be ashamed of. You didn't do anything wrong.* None of that sinks in when the prosecutor is telling you to be prepared for questions about your sexual history and when well-meaning people practically run from the room if anything close to the topic comes up. My sexual history had been remarkably bland in the big scheme, but it was amazing to see how things could get twisted.

So yeah, I'd wanted Joe to suffer as much as I had, yet I'd known it was impossible for that to ever happen. Four long years later, Joe got hit. Twice. Wow. It felt strangely good to know that even though I also knew it didn't come close to what he'd done to me. Alex ran a hand through his already mussed hair and let out a sigh before looking over at me. He set his mug on the coffee table and leaned his elbows on his knees. "I'm sorry. I've made a bloody mess for you," he said, his words earnest and pained.

I stared at him. I felt energized, buzzing with a strange elation and buoyed by the heat coursing through me. I set my coffee beside his on the table and rocked up on my knees. Not giving him a chance to stop me, I placed a palm on his chest and pushed him back, immediately straddling him. His eyes widened, but he didn't resist.

"What are you apologizing for? The worst happened four years ago. Maybe it's not right, but I don't care. I'm glad you hit him."

He stared at me, his intent gaze doing funny things to my insides. "Okay," he said slowly. "Here's hoping it doesn't get too much press."

I skipped past that worry and shrugged. "Can't be too bad, right?"

He lifted one shoulder in a light shrug. "Guess we'll find out. Harper, what..."

His breath drew in sharply when I settled my hips against him and traced a finger along his jaw. I'd never really paid much attention to a guy's face. Oh, I'd have said I was attracted to the guys I'd dated, back when I actually dated. Since then, I could say I'd notice a man was handsome here and there, but it was in a detached sense. With Alex, all it had taken was a few minutes alone with him and he'd gone from an objectively handsome man to burn-me-up, melt-me-down sexy. I wanted to gobble him up. The air around us hummed to life. That buzzy feeling inside bumped into the heat Alex set aflame inside, and I couldn't think past anything other than wanting him.

I followed the strong line of his jaw and trailed my fingers down his neck, savoring the hard beat of his pulse there. His gaze darkened, and I could feel his eyes on me, sparks striking under my skin everywhere his eyes landed. Heat pooled low in my belly, and my pulse ran fast and shallow. I slipped my hand around his neck and into his rumpled brown hair.

I could feel his cock hardening, the pressure right where I wanted it. I rocked my hips subtly, watching when he closed his eyes. His gaze pierced me when he lifted his eyelids. "Harper, what are you doing?" he asked, his voice strained.

"This."

I ran my hands roughly down his chest and slid them up under his shirt, almost moaning at the feel of his skin, hot over the hard planes of his abdomen. I rolled my hips again, savoring the little spike of pleasure from where his hard cock rubbed against my clit. The two layers of denim between us only served to heighten my need.

His breath came out in a half-groan. He gripped my hands in his, stilling them. "I don't know if this is..."

I knew where he was going, and I didn't like it. "Don't you dare say this isn't a good time. Whatever. Nothing that happened today should change anything. Don't you dare try to act like I need to be treated carefully. I don't." My words came out fast and fierce. Anger flashed inside, hot on its heels was the burning need I felt. I stared back at him. Whatever he saw there, his gaze shifted from contained to just plain hot, so hot, my channel clenched at the look there.

He moved swiftly, gripping my hips and holding me against him as he arched into me, before hooking his hand under the edge of my shirt and lifting it off in one swoop. It sailed to the floor, landing in a soft rumple. His palm swept up my back in a heated pass, pulling me to him. He took my lips in a fierce kiss. There was no hesitation. He met my reckless need with his own. Our kiss was rough, deep and wet. Meanwhile, his hands roved over my body. I didn't want soft and slow. I needed more to slake the restless need beating inside me like a drum, drowning out everything but the feel of Alex against me. My bra was thrown aside, and he rolled my nipples between his fingers before sucking one into his mouth and driving me near to insanity with licks and nips as he alternated between them.

I managed to yank his shirt off somewhere along the way, savoring the feel of his hardness in contrast to my softness. My hips had a mind of their own, rocking against him, chasing after the sharp streaks of pleasure with the friction between us. He muttered against my skin where he'd been leaving a wet trail of kisses between my breasts and lifted his head.

"Bloody hell, Harper. You're driving me mad."

He lifted me off of him and yanked my jeans open, shoving them down roughly. I kicked my legs free and went to return the favor. He let out a rough groan, the sound alone pebbling my skin and tightening my nipples, when I freed his cock and curled my palm around its hot, velvety length. Any thought I'd had about drawing this out fled. I needed him inside of me. Now. I moved to straddle him where he sat with his jeans open and barely off his hips.

"Not so fast."

Once again, he was quick. His hand curled around my hip and held me still. Before I had a chance to speak, he leaned forward and slid a finger through my folds. I was so wet, the insides of my thighs were damp. My knees almost buckled, and I gasped when he nudged my thighs apart with his knee and sank a finger knuckle-deep inside of me.

I looked down and couldn't take my eyes away as another finger joined the first, stroking in and out. I was so close to release, little shocks of pleasure hit me in waves. Just when I thought I might die from the need to find release, he drew his fingers out and dipped his head, dragging his tongue across my clit—once, just once. Just enough to nearly send my flying. He leaned back, his hot gaze on me, as he yanked his wallet out of his pocket. Tugging a condom out sent his wallet tumbling to the floor. He smoothed it on with one hand.

So frantic to have him inside, I was straddling him inside of a second. Yet again, he held me back, both of his strong hands gripping my hips. Restless, I rocked into him, a little moan escaping at the feel of his cock, so hard and hot, sliding against my folds.

"Harper. Look at me."

I whipped my eyes open to find his waiting—dark and intent, a fierce tenderness there that grabbed me by the heart. I felt suddenly vulnerable, the depth of need beating between us running so hot and fast I couldn't ignore it.

He eased his grip on my hip and reached

between us, positioning his cock at my entrance. In one surge, he flexed up as I sank down, crying out at the feel of him filling me. I couldn't look away, his magnetic gaze held mine as we started to rock together. My skin was damp, my breasts rubbing lightly against his chest as we moved. I loved how strong he felt, how fluid every motion was. He rocked deeper and deeper into me, letting me set the pace. I lost myself in the rhythm, lost myself in the moment of joining with him. Pressure gathered within, spiraling tighter and tighter until I was teetering and breathless. He stroked between us, sliding his thumb across the slick nub of my desire, and sent me flying. Pleasure arrowed through me, little shocks reverberating as I drifted down. He held me against him as he drove deeply one last time and then shuddered, emitting a rough groan as his head fell forward into the dip of my shoulder.

I curled against him when he slipped his arms around me and rested there in his embrace. Right then, I didn't want to move. Ever.

Chapter Thirteen

ALEX

I could feel Harper's heart beating against my chest, the rhythm fast and steady, matching my own. She was relaxed against me, and it felt so fucking good to hold her I didn't want to move. My heartbeat gradually slowed as we sat there. I felt her skin pebble against mine and reluctantly lifted my head.

"You're cold. Let's get you warm."

She opened her eyes on a sigh. "I don't want to move," she said with a small smile.

"That makes two of us, but no sense in you getting chilly."

I heard motion behind us and realized Stanley must've woken from his nap over in the corner. Another moment passed and his distinctive steps reached us, his cold nose bumping my hand.

Harper giggled, and I was beyond relieved she wasn't tensing up. The other night had been mind-blowing and sublime, but I hadn't forgotten how she'd gotten edgy afterwards. We'd had the convenience of a late hour and a bed we were already in to make it easy to curl around her and go to sleep. Now though, it was only late afternoon with the sun shining through the clouds outside and into her living room. If Stanley being nosy would keep her from starting to think too much, that was fine with me.

It wasn't that I didn't want her to think at all. More that I didn't want her to start worrying. I sensed she was on questioning ground when it came to us. I figured she had plenty of reason for that, so I was prepared to be patient. She leaned back and looked at me. Lifting a hand, she ran it through my hair. "Let's shower," she said suddenly.

"Whatever you want," I replied, meaning it on multiple levels.

A shower sounded perfect. It would chase away Harper's chill. She carefully climbed off my lap, and I missed the feel of her instantly. I gave myself a mental shake and stood, following her into the bathroom off of her bedroom. She had a half-bath beside the living room and a rather luxurious bathroom adjacent to her bedroom with a large oval-shaped bathtub and a walk-in shower.

I tossed my condom in the trash and kicked my jeans off, following her into the steamy shower. I was quickly discovering that any time Harper was near me, my body was on notice. It didn't matter that I'd just spent myself inside of her. Nope. I took one look at her—her skin slick under the water with soap running all over her—and I wanted her again.

I shackled my needs and took the soap from her when she handed it to me. I couldn't manage to keep my hand from sliding down her back and over the curve of her bottom.

———

Monday rolled around, and as instructed by Coach, I met him at his office for a meeting with a lawyer after practice. At my knock, he called for me to come in. I stepped inside to see him at his desk as usual, idly tossing a mini basketball in a hoop mounted to the wall beside his desk. Coach wasn't one to sit still. He had a variety of fidget toys on his desk and was usually playing with one of them. He glanced up at me with a smile.

"You're doing better at blocking shots in the far left corner," he said by way of greeting.

The far, upper left corner of the net was the one and only place a few goals had slipped past me last season. As such, Coach had assigned the offensive players to attack that corner every time we practiced. End result: only one goal had gotten past me this season. I threw him a grin. "That's the plan, eh?"

"That it is." The ball swished through the hoop and bounced back into his hands. He set it on the desk and spun to face me. "Okay, let's deal with the mess. Management sent a lawyer our way, but forgot to give me a name. We have attorneys on staff, but criminal defense isn't what we hire them for. Whoever this lawyer is will be here in a few minutes. You either have more sense than most, or you're really good at playing it cool. Which one is it?"

I shook my head, puzzled. "I'm not sure what you mean."

Coach barked a laugh. "More sense. If you'd listened to or read the news, I figured you might not be too happy about it."

Truth be told, I didn't pay much attention to the news, at least not anything that even brushed up against gossip. I'd seen the damage it did to teammates before, so I mostly tried to live a life that was so damn boring, I wouldn't even blip on the radar. I wasn't so stupid as to think punching a guy on the sidewalk wouldn't be news for a player on our team, I was just studiously avoiding thinking about it. There was the fact I didn't want to worry about something I couldn't control, and I preferred to focus on Harper. I was doing my damnedest not to interpret too much, but I'd lucked into another night with her after being all but ordered over to Liam's for Olivia to chew me out.

Olivia was none too happy about what had happened, although in between every sentence, she kept saying how much Joe deserved to get punched. Liam finally interrupted and pointed that out, only to get a pillow thrown at him. I sat through her lecture because I knew why she was worried. Harper sure as hell didn't need anyone to stir up the past for her, and I'd gone and done it.

I looked over at Coach and ran a hand through my hair, still damp from my shower after practice. "Figured it wouldn't do me a bit of good to pay attention to the news. Anything I need to do about it?"

Coach leaned back in his chair and shrugged. "Meet with the lawyer and hopefully get those charges dropped. The media is completely shocked because you're supposed to be the good lad from Britain. Good news is they've already dug up Joe Schmidt's past, so he's not looking too rosy. Bad news is your girlfriend was mentioned too. I had our PR guy check on the past stories because they don't usually name victims when it comes to rape cases. Sad to say, she was named before because he released her name to the press and claimed the sex was consensual. Guy's a damn asshole of the highest order," Coach said flatly.

I stared at him, anger rolling through me in a flash. All I had were the outlines of what happened to Harper. Even when I'd gone to look up Joe, I hadn't bothered to review all the stories from that time. I'd missed the details of why she'd been named publicly. Hard to admit, but I hadn't thought much about how that came to be. I hadn't ever considered the ramifications of someone in Harper's situation before. I doubt many men liked to think about what it meant to be raped. Men were the lucky ones in the sense we didn't have to worry about it much, not the way women did. Olivia had pointedly told me that most women had at least one friend who'd been through it. Hearing that Joe had been behind Harper's name becoming public made me furious. I didn't realize I was clenching my fists until Coach spoke.

"Calm down, Alex. Not a damn thing you can do about that. Honestly, he deserved a helluva lot more than a few blows to the face, but you can't change the past. I've got our PR guys on it. They're leaning hard to spin this for what it was. A good guy finally giving an asshole what he deserved. Now we just need to see what we can do about those charges. Let's be clear: I'm not saying what you did was a good choice. Fists don't usually solve anything. I'm just saying I understand how you felt."

I stretched my hands open and took a slow breath before nodding. "Right. I know it won't help, but bloody hell. It's just…" I stopped, emotion knotting in my chest. It was so fucking unfair what had happened. None of it was right, and I wanted to make it so.

Coach's gaze held mine, a flicker of something in the depths. "Life is most certainly not fair. Best thing you can do is be there for her," he said gruffly.

I knew Coach had his own share of tragedy. He'd been flying high as one of the best footballers in the world when he was in a car accident with his wife and daughter. He lived, and they didn't. He was hobbled by his injuries and never played again. He lost his family and his career in one day. I knew he knew precisely how unfair life could be. I met his eyes and nodded, unable to speak just yet.

At that moment, there was a knock at the door. At Coach's call, a woman stepped briskly into his office. She strode straight to Coach's desk. She was tall and imposing, her presence so strong I stood reflexively. She had to be close to six feet tall with auburn hair pulled back into a sleek knot and hazel eyes. I realized how far gone I was over Harper when all I could manage was a dispassionate acknowledgment that she was beautiful, if a little intimidating. What with her height and strong presence, she commanded attention and seriousness.

"Zoe Lawson," she said, holding a hand out.

Her handshake was confident, firm and businesslike, just like her presence. After introductions, Coach gestured for her to sit in the chair beside me. We collectively sat, and Zoe immediately opened a file folder tucked under her elbow. Her sharp gaze swung to me. "Well, the good part is you'll definitely win the publicity war here. You were avenging your girlfriend. No one will think you're the jerk in this story. The bad part is you punched Mr. Schmidt twice in front of multiple witnesses, and you happen to be a public figure, so plenty of people recognized you. I've reviewed everything. I need to know how hard you want to fight the charges before we decide how to proceed."

Zoe closed the file folder and set it on the edge of Coach's desk before looking my way again. I was still absorbing the fact that first Coach and now Zoe had called Harper my girlfriend. I liked it. Quite a lot. Yet, I wasn't so sure that's what she was, nor how she viewed what was happening with us. I forced my thoughts onto the matter at hand.

"I guess I didn't even think about fighting the charges. I mean, it definitely happened. I'm not about to lie about it," I said.

Zoe barely smiled and flicked her eyes to Coach. "What would the team like to see happen? You're in the unfortunate position of having an honest player here." Her gaze bounced to me. "No offense, but I'm used to dealing with sports stars who have some trumped up story about how someone walked into their fist, or whatever details need to fit what happened. I appreciate how honest you are, but as a criminal defense at-torney, clients like you can make my job more challenging," she said with a slight shake of her head.

Coach chuckled. "Alex *is* honest, and I'd like him to stay that way. How about you give us some feedback on how to proceed knowing that's he's the guy he is?"

I stayed quiet, but it was nice to know Coach appreciated me for who I was. Truth was, plenty of athletes were assholes behind their public façade. The media fawning al-lowed that to happen, and it was bloody an-noying. It was good to have a Coach who had no tolerance for rubbish like that.

Zoe drummed her fingertips on the arm-rest of her chair for a moment and shrugged. "We'll play it straight, but play up his history and what Mr. Schmidt said before you punched him."

She slipped the file folder closer on the desk and opened it. "According to your police interview, he referred to Harper as an old friend. Then when you asked him if that's what he called the women he raped, he said 'Fuck you.' Sound accurate?"

"It's what happened and what I told the police," I replied, wondering why she was repeating the obvious.

She closed the folder again. "Repetition is critical. I don't doubt you for a second, but you need to get used to being asked the same questions again and again. I'm hoping we don't even go to trial, but if we do, trust me, don't get annoyed with being asked to repeat what happened a few hundred times."

I bit back a sigh and ran a hand through my hair. I might not regret punching Joe. In fact, learning he was responsible to making Harper's name public before only made me want to do it again, but it didn't mean I wanted to deal with this circus. "Right then. Will do."

"How likely you think it is he'll go to trial?" Coach asked.

Zoe looked to him and shrugged. "Not very likely if the press keeps hammering the angle they already have. You look like the hero against a rapist who managed to barely serve any time."

"But how does that help with the fact I hit him?" I asked.

"The longer this stays in the news, the

more Mr. Schmidt has to be back in the public eye. I doubt he realizes it because guys like him usually don't, but he got lucky before. I reviewed his court records. My guess is if Ms. Jacobs had wanted to keep dealing with a dragged out court case, he would've been convicted for the original charges, and she'd have been dragged through hell to make it happen. Rape cases are ugly for the victims. They have to testify about something terrible, reliving it over and over, and deal with cross-examination while they're at it. It's extremely unpleasant and the reason something like only three-percent of rape cases ever go to trial. I wasn't there at the time, but I imagine the prosecutor offered a plea deal because Mr. Schmidt had a very aggressive defense attorney who was prepared to make it as ugly as possible for Ms. Jacobs. He got off easy. Now the whole sordid story is back in the news and he looks like the asshole he is. Not good for his professional reputation at all. He works in finance. I would bet his job might be at risk now because they won't want any association with a former rapist who just called his victim an old friend. As far as I'm concerned, you let your PR team blow this up. Mr. Schmidt might end up wishing he'd never pressed charges against you. Does that mean it will completely disappear? No. Too many witnesses, but we can agree to a deal that probably means community service for you," Zoe said with a firm nod.

Coach said something in reply, and they continued talking while my thoughts spun off wondering just how bloody awful the lead up to the plea deal must have been for Harper after Joe was charged. I didn't like thinking about it. At all. In fact, thinking about it only made me angry again. Bloody hell. I'd been angry more ever since Olivia dropped this little bomb on me than I had since I was a lad. I'd thought my problems with my temper long gone.

Coach cleared his throat, and I looked back over at him. He leaned back in his chair and angled his head to the side. "You're pissed again," he said calmly.

I bit back a sigh and shrugged. "I don't like hearing about what Harper went through. I especially don't like thinking about how easy Joe got off. It's a load of bollocks is what it is."

Zoe looked at me calmly and shrugged. "It certainly is, but don't throw your fists around anymore, okay? We can handle this situation without too much trouble. If it happens again, you won't look as sympathetic as you do now."

Bloody hell. She was practical. I swallowed the next curse I wanted to spit out and closed my eyes while I took a deep breath instead. Opening them, I glanced between her and Coach. "No worries about me."

Zoe nodded and stood, snagging the file folder and tucking it under her elbow again. "Well, I'll be in touch after I speak with the prosecutor tomorrow. In the meantime, make your life as boring as possible," she said with such a slight smile, it was barely noticeable.

She strode out of Coach's office, her footsteps echoing on the tiled floor as she walked down the hallway. Coach stood and closed his office door, returning to lean his hips against the side of his desk. He eyed me for several beats. "It's okay to be angry about something, you know."

I stared back at him, wrestling with my own thoughts. Intellectually, I knew there was good reason to be angry with Joe. Yet, years of watching my father rule with anger had set me up to curb mine. I finally shrugged, uncertain where Coach meant to go with his comment.

"I'm only saying that because I haven't seen you anything other than calm in the year plus you've been playing with the team. That's a damn good thing. Your steadiness is a huge part of what keeps the team focused in tough games. I can't say why, but you seem rattled by getting angry over this situation with Harper. You should be pissed. Hell, I'm pissed. Thing is, when people get angry and think they shouldn't be angry, that's when they do dumb things like punch people on the street because they've been too busy stuffing their anger."

At that, he pushed off the side of his desk. "I'll call you as soon as I hear anything back from Zoe. You do the same if you hear from her. Okay?"

"Of course. See you tomorrow at practice."

As I made me way out of the stadium, I considered Coach's comment. I hadn't thought much about whether I'd been stuffing any of my anger when it came to what happened to Harper. I didn't like being angry and especially didn't like feeling so helpless. As Coach so plainly said, I couldn't change the past.

Chapter Fourteen

HARPER

"Bye Stanley," I said, giving his sleek head a pet. "Be back later."

He nudged my leg and turned to amble over to his favorite napping spot in the corner where a splash of sun fell through the windows. I'd awoken to an overcast morning and gone for a run with Alex in the light drizzle. When it came to Alex, my thoughts were a jumble. I was starting to feel half-crazy because I wanted to see him all the time, but that didn't fit with what I'd thought would happen with him. Not that I'd ever known what it would be like to finally break through the wall I'd built around myself and actually desire someone again. I wasn't prepared for thinking about Alex nearly all the time and aching to see him again. I looked forward to our morning runs together because I knew I was guaranteed a solid hour in his presence. I wanted a hell of a lot more than that, but I was in the midst of my own internal battle over what to do about that.

My hard won peace of mind was coming to seem more superficial than I'd hoped. It relied on me avoiding emotionally charged situations, something I hadn't discovered I'd been avoiding until Alex came along. Much as a part of me was near desperate to wrap myself in everything that was Alex, allowing that to happen meant letting go in a way I hadn't in years. Honestly, in a way I'd never let go emotionally. The scorching intimacy I experienced with Alex was like nothing I'd ever experienced.

I gave my head a shake and slipped my jacket on, glancing over to see Stanley already sound asleep in his little patch of sun. Sometime between getting home from our run and my shower, the light drizzle had stopped and the sun was playing peek-a-boo through the clouds. I locked the door behind me and headed out to work.

I'd fallen in love with my new apartment when I saw it for several reasons. The windows offered a view of Puget Sound in the distance, it was on the same side of town as Daisy and Olivia, and it was closer to my job. I'd loved the fact it was close to a park as well because that meant a good place for walks with Stanley. I hadn't considered running into Joe because I couldn't have known he lived nearby. I still didn't know anything other than that he went running in the park and I'd seen him in his car. Even the knowledge of his presence couldn't puncture the warmth I felt now that Alex was in my life.

Well, I suppose he'd been in my life before. Ever since Olivia had moved in with Liam, Alex had been on the periphery of my life. I'd see him whenever Olivia and Liam had gatherings with friends. It hadn't escaped my notice Alex was all kinds of sexy bundled up in an amazing body, but he'd kept his distance enough that I hadn't seen beyond the surface. Truth be told, I hadn't paid much attention to any man. It was strange to consider it, but the collision of encountering Alex in the park and seeing Joe at the same time had snapped me out of a numb place inside.

Just thinking about Alex now sent a flash of heat rolling through me. I turned on the radio, only to hear Alex's name. Even though

I knew it might be something I didn't want to hear, I turned up the volume.

.... Alex Gordon's recent charges are a shock in Seattle. Gordon is known for never losing his cool and has never even been called for a foul during his pro soccer career. Until this, he was clean as a whistle and considered Britain's gentleman footballer. He's facing assault charges against Joe Schmidt, the former track star previously charged with rape against a female runner who was ranked nationally during her college career. There was public outcry over the paltry sentence Mr. Schmidt agreed to in a plea deal, serving only a few months of time. Reports indicate Gordon is involved with Mr. Schmidt's victim. Gordon looks like the hero here. Fans are saying Gordon did it for love.

The radio announcer continued and then shifted into a discussion on a local sports news station. I switched the radio off, my stomach churning. I couldn't say I hadn't been prepared. Alex himself had tried to tell me he was worried about this very thing. I guess I'd just shoved it away, thinking it couldn't be that interesting to anyone. But then, I'd done the same thing back when Joe raped me. I'd been completely unprepared for the media attention and devastated when Joe announced my name during a live interview. The press had kept my name out of it until then. After that, every publication with any decency had actually called to ask if I preferred they continued to withhold my name, but I'd told them it didn't matter. Because it didn't. Joe had already done his damage, and shoving my name back into anonymity had been impossible at that point. I only prayed this would blow over quickly.

I zipped into my parking spot at my office and jogged inside. I liked my job, I really did. I kind of fell into it, but physical therapy turned out to be a good fit for me. My senior year in college had been a blur. I'd barely been able to focus and my grades had slipped. I had to spend an extra year in classes recouping from that mess. My track coach had been kind enough to set me up with a job providing support to the physical therapy team for various collegiate programs. I'd enjoyed it because the job itself offered opportunities for me to stay fit, and I enjoyed helping others. Sad to say, but part of the appeal at the time had been free access to the on-site gyms. I'd been deep in the echoes of fear from Joe's attack and had been too scared to run outside at the time. Yet, I'd craved the physical burn of working out and the escape it offered me.

I'd gradually worked up to walks outside

with Stanley, but had only started running outside again with Alex. Another gift he'd given me—of such import it was hard to convey. I waved at the receptionist and headed down the hall to my office. I still worked at the university occasionally, but my official job was with a clinic that provided physical therapy and orthopedic consults all over Seattle. Olivia and I sometimes referred to each other with her being an orthopedic surgeon. I liked the freedom of my position and the ability to see a wide range of patients.

I stepped into my office to find Daisy waiting in one of the chairs by my desk. "Hey there, what are you doing here?" I asked, puzzled at her appearance.

Daisy twirled the ends of her blonde ponytail in her fingers and shrugged. "Just thought I'd say hi."

While it wasn't completely unusual for Daisy to drop in, she was too nonchalant for that. I hung my jacket and leaned my hips on the desk. "You're not here just to say hi. You're checking on me, aren't you?"

Daisy sighed and wrinkled her nose. "So how are you?"

I pondered her question seriously. I wasn't great. It wasn't good to know Alex was in the news and the biggest ghost of my past was in the public eye again because of what had happened. Yet, I'd come a long way. I was unsettled and anxious, but I felt okay. I didn't have that old panicky feeling where I felt strewn into broken pieces inside, always trying to put myself back together and never quite able to pull it off. Oddly, I wanted to see Alex. I wasn't quite ready to examine what that might mean, but somehow the thought of seeing him made me feel better. He was someone to hold onto, and I didn't doubt for a second he'd be there if I asked.

I met Daisy's concerned gaze. "I'm really okay. Were you driving in and heard the same thing I did?"

She rolled her eyes and sighed. "Yes. It got me worried. But you look… Well, you look okay. Want to grab some lunch today?"

"Sure. How about…" I leaned back and glanced at my schedule. The receptionist printed it for me everyday and left it on my desk even though I had it in my phone calendar. "12:30?"

"Perfect. I'll meet you here." Daisy stood and gave me a swift hug before leaving with a wave.

I jumped into work, relieved I had a busy schedule this morning. If anything could take my mind off of the treadmill of worry and anxiety, staying busy could. I worked with an elderly woman who was a few months into her recovery from a broken hip and moved onto a session with a professional body-builder who'd torn his rotator cuff. The contrast between the two was so stark as to be amusing. Janet, the elderly woman who'd fallen, had me cheering as she showed off her walking skills. I had just returned to my office from the gym to check on a few things when my desk phone rang. I answered without bothering to check to see who was calling.

"Ms. Jacobs, Brad Williams from the Seattle Observer here. I'm calling with regard to the incident with Alex Gordon and to discuss whether you have any comment on the matter."

I stared at the phone. As innocuous as it looked, at the moment, I wanted to throw the phone across the room. On the heels of my anger came dread. I silently cursed myself. I should've known the media would call. I should've been prepared for this. I just hadn't wanted to think about it. At all. My life had rolled past this, and I didn't want to wade back into the quagmire.

"Ms. Jacobs?"

I opened my mouth to speak, out of reflex and the habit of manners, before I snapped it shut. I didn't have to talk to anyone. I started to hang up when I considered that might not help me. If I wanted any say in how this played out, I couldn't hide from it. To this day, I wondered if I hadn't been so ready to curl up and hide if I'd have had the endurance to go through a trial. Because that's what it required—enduring the indignity of replaying the worst moments of my life and the shame in which they were cloaked. I'd been too tired and still reeling from the shock of it all to face it. Maybe I couldn't go back in time and rectify that, but perhaps I could affect how this played out. I took a deep breath, gathering my courage, and tried to quell the fast pounding of my heart.

"Yes. I'm here," I finally managed.

The reporter cleared his throat. "Okay, well, I think I'm glad you didn't hang up on me," he replied.

His tone was polite and careful, yet there was just enough warmth in it, I sensed I could trust him, at least enough to talk for a few minutes. "I was thinking about it," I said, the bald truth coming out before I reconsidered my words.

"Can't say I blame you. Well, now that I

have you, do you mind taking a few minutes to answer some questions?"

"How about you ask, and if I feel comfortable answering, I will?"

"Works for me."

There was another pause. "Would it be more comfortable if I came to meet with you in person?"

I spun in my desk chair to look out the windows. The clinic where I worked was in downtown Seattle with our offices on the third floor of a larger building, offering a view of the Seattle skyline with Puget Sound in the distance. I watched as a red-tailed hawk flew past my window to land on the wide sill jutting out from the windows. A pair of hawks nested there every year, and everyone in the office enjoyed keeping an eye on them. My gut was churning and my heart was pounding in a clangy, shallow beat—that's how it felt whenever I was anxious. I didn't know if I was half crazy to even have this conversation, but I figured in person would be better because I'd have a better sense of the reporter.

"I'd like that." I glanced up at the clock. I had an hour before Daisy would be here to meet me for lunch and an unexpected opening in my schedule due to a cancellation.

"If you can meet me now, I have an hour," I said quickly before I chickened out.

———

Brad Williams sat across from me at the small round table in my office roughly ten minutes later. I didn't know where he'd come from, but he'd made it to the clinic within minutes. He was a whip-thin man with silver hair, sharp blue eyes and glasses. He had a somber, thoughtful air to him. It wouldn't have surprised me to learn he was a runner. He had the build and energy for it. We'd gotten through the pleasantries, and he presently had a cup of coffee from our waiting area in hand.

He looked over at me and cocked his head to the side. "You might want to know I was one of the lead reporters for the Observer back when Mr. Schmidt was charged with rape and assault. I'm also an alumni from his university and ran for the track team there back in my day."

"Oh, really? Did I speak with you before?" I asked. My memories of the calls from reporters during those few months after my name had been made public and the case finally dropped off the radar after his plea deal were blurry. I hadn't met with anyone in person.

Brad held my gaze for a moment before nodding. "We spoke on the phone once. You may not remember, but the Observer chose not to use your name in our reporting even after it had been disclosed publicly."

The knot of tension in the pit of my stomach coiled a little tighter. "I don't remember that, but I tried not to read about it," I said with a shrug.

"Understood." He took a sip of coffee and glanced to the recorder he'd set between us on the table. He'd asked if he could use it, and I'd agreed on the condition he send me anything for review before it was published. He set his coffee down and looked square at me. "Well, let's start with the basics. Any comment on the charges against Mr. Gordon?"

"I suppose all I have to say is I understand why it happened. I don't mean to say hitting someone is a good idea, just that he was upset and it's what happened."

"It's safe to say plenty of people agree with you on that. Can you tell me the nature of your relationship to Mr. Gordon?"

My heart set to banging in my chest. I had anticipated this question, but I still didn't know how to answer it. I felt my cheeks heating. Alex had quickly come to mean far more than I'd expected. In the span of a few weeks, he'd gone through several stages in what he meant to me. A casual friend who I trusted because of his connection to a dear friend. I trusted Olivia completely and by extension Liam. Liam held Alex in the highest esteem and considered him his best friend, so even before I'd gotten to know Alex better, I'd trusted him by virtue of those connections alone. He'd then become a man I wanted with a ferocity that knocked through my self-imposed defenses and made me feel alive again. Yet, even in the headiness of that desire, I'd had a single goal and it was purely physical. I couldn't have known acting on that would kick things up another notch. I hadn't anticipated the feeling of connection with him, an intimacy raw and startling in its depth.

I abruptly wished I'd thought to call Alex before I met with Brad. For a second, I started to worry I might say the wrong thing. The worry vanished as suddenly as it manifested because I knew with certainty that Alex wouldn't hold anything I said against me even if it created problems for him and his case.

"He's a good friend," I said. The moment the words came out, I reconsidered. "He might be more than that," I blurted out next, wishing instantly I could take the words back, not because of the circumstances under which I said them, but because everything with Alex felt too new, too raw—fragile as spun sugar.

Brad merely nodded and took another sip of coffee, conveniently oblivious to how much it meant that I was even allowing myself to think about a man in any context with me that wasn't purely platonic.

My office door opened simultaneous with a knock, and Daisy stood there. She had a tense look to her, her eyes flicking from me to Brad. She put her hands on her hips and slammed the door shut behind her, her gaze locked on Brad. "Don't you dare make her..."

I held a hand up. "Daisy, it's okay. I told him I would meet with him."

Her concerned gaze bounced to me. "What are you thinking?"

"That I'd rather have my own say about it than to have people speculating."

She pursed her lips, and I felt heartened at her appearance. Even if it was unnecessary at the moment, it was good to have Daisy in my corner. She was fierce when it came to protecting her friends. She glanced between us and promptly pulled out a chair.

"Okay, consider me, I don't know, her... her friend who will kick your ass if needed," she said with a firm nod.

Brad flashed a small grin. "Fair enough. Mind if I ask you a question?"

"Go for it," Daisy replied firmly.

"Any comment on the situation?"

"Joe deserved it. That's exactly what I think."

Brad angled his head to the side. "Perhaps you could elaborate on why you think that?"

Daisy leaned forward, her brown eyes fairly snapping with anger. "He raped and assaulted my friend. Even if she wasn't my friend, I'd have been horrified by what he did. He made the court case into a living hell for her, making it not worth going through a trial, and he got off way too easy if you ask me. Karma's like a boomerang and sometimes it takes longer for it to come around, but it always does. A few punches doesn't even come close to what he put Harper through, so he should still consider himself lucky."

I almost laughed, not because it was funny, but rather the overwhelming relief made me giddy and the circumstances of this particular moment bordered on ludicrous.

Brad and Daisy continued talking while my attention started to wander a bit. Until Daisy said... "Well, I mean it's obvious Alex did it for love."

My head whipped in her direction, my heart starting to bang wildly in my chest, and hope waving a little flag and dancing inside. I promptly ignored hope's attention-seeking gambit. The last thing I needed was to start getting all wistful over what might be. Daisy was definitely on the passionate side when it came to her feelings. She felt everything strongly, and tended to assume the same of everyone. "Daisy, I don't know..."

She waved a hand dismissively in my direction. "You can be all coy about it, but it's not going to change anything. He wouldn't have been so angry if he didn't really care about you."

"Yeah but, I don't think..."

Brad caught my eye and shook his head. "Don't worry. I won't be announcing Mr. Gordon's in love with you. Well, unless he tells me so," he said with another slight smile.

Daisy crossed her legs, one foot bouncing up and down. "Oh whatever. You should let it be a good story. Maybe I'm getting ahead of myself with the whole love thing, but you have to admit he's way into you."

I blushed so hard, I could've used some cold water to splash on my face. I couldn't quite believe we were having this conversation in front of a reporter, but then Daisy was never one to shy away from anything. I looked to Brad. "Did you have any more questions for me?"

"Just one: do you have any concerns that Mr. Schmidt is a risk to other women?"

His question took me aback, but only for a second. I knew the answer without hesitation. "Of course. He never took responsibility for what he did even when he accepted the plea deal. I've always wondered if it would happen again."

Chapter Fifteen

ALEX

I breathed in the cool, rainy air and slowed my stride as we approached the entrance to the park. Harper was still meeting me daily to run. Honestly, I had tried to run every day before, but practice was enough of a workout that I'd skip here and there. With Harper, I hadn't missed a day. Another two weeks had passed since I'd landed my fist in Joe's face and not much had really happened with that. Zoe kept Coach and I apprised of her communication with the prosecutor, but beyond the initial filing of charges, nothing had changed. She'd filed something to delay something—hell, she told me what, but it was in dry, legal terms so I didn't absorb it— and told us she preferred to take a wait and see approach. She thought Joe might back off if he got too much public pressure. I kept reminding her I had actually punched him, but she shrugged it off.

Meanwhile, I was doing my damnedest to ignore the press, while Coach was busy stirring it up. He didn't seem to care what the status of my charges was. He was focused on the whole 'good guy Seattle Stars player' press. Harper had told me about her call from the reporter from the Seattle Observer and showed me the story he wrote. I figured it was her call to say whatever she wanted, but it sure seemed like the reporter had some lingering opinions on what happened with Joe's old case. He spent half of the article reviewing the light sentence Joe got and comparing it to average sentences for the crimes he'd pled to. Oh, it bloody pissed me off that rape wasn't on that list, but Joe was stuck with assault charges.

The good thing in all this: I got to see Harper more. Beyond our morning runs, I'd stolen another two nights with her. I glanced to her as we transitioned to a walk once we reached the sidewalk beyond the park entrance. Like me, she eschewed a raincoat when we ran in the rain, insisting it was annoying to listen to the rustle of it and she didn't mind getting wet. Her dark brown hair was wet with a loose lock sticking to her cheek. Without thinking, I reached over and brushed it off her cheek. She glanced to me, her blue eyes bright in the silvery gray light.

Just like that, I was hard. The air around us felt electrified. I almost stumbled, too busy staring at her when we reached a cross street that I didn't notice I was stepping off the sidewalk.

"Alex!"

She grabbed my arm just as a car whizzed by. Bloody hell. This woman made me lose my mind and definitely my focus. We stood there with her hand curled around my forearm and the misty rain falling all around us. Cars passed by, one rolling through a puddle nearby and sending a splash of water on our legs. The splash penetrated the fog in my brain, and I finally tore my gaze away. I shook my arm loose, curled my hand around hers and started walking. I had one thing on my mind. I needed Harper. Now.

Our route through the park this morning landed us closer to my flat on the way back. It was a bloody good thing Harper seemed to be of the same mind as me because otherwise I'd have been practically dragging her. As it was, we were almost running when we reached the steps to my building. Usually, I'd stop the check on Callie, but not today. We made it through my front door in seconds, and I spun around the moment the door slammed shut behind us.

We were both drenched. My t-shirt was sticking to my skin, as was hers. That worked for me because her nipples were tight peaks through her bra and shirt. When she looked up at me as she leaned against the door, a drop of rain rolled down her cheek and onto her neck. I dipped my head and licked it off. Just that small taste of her skin and lust bolted through me.

Our lips collided in a hot, wet, messy kiss. I wanted to devour her, frantic to slake the need pounding through me. Seeing her daily kept me in a state of semi-constant arousal, all the while I was trying not to force myself into her life. Liam had told me enough times I could be intense, so I'd been trying to tone it down and let the course of what was happening between us unfold gradually. Bloody hell. It was the hardest thing I'd ever done. The only time I wasn't batting thoughts of her away was during practice and games.

Harper's tongue dueled with mine and she nipped at my lips, an edge of wildness to her that matched my own. Her skin was cool and damp and pebbled under my touch. Her head thumped against the door when I stepped back and dragged her wet t-shirt over her head, her bra following in quick succession. Her nipples, dusky pink and damp, tempted me as they tightened further in the cool air, but she didn't give me a chance to draw one into my mouth when she yanked at my shirt, sliding her hands up underneath and stepping closer to me.

I reached behind my head and tugged my shirt away where it fell to the floor in a rumple with hers. Before I had a chance to think, her lips were mapping their way down my chest as she shoved my shorts down, immediately curling her palm around my cock when it bounced free from my briefs. My knees almost gave way at the feel of her stroking me. I was pushed up against the edge of my control and so hard, I was on the verge of pain.

Her lips kept mapping their way down, and I groaned when she dragged her tongue along the underside of my cock. She shimmied down to her knees, and I gripped her damp hair, powerless to stop her when she set to explore every inch of my shaft with her lips and tongue. By the time she drew me into her warm mouth, I was about to explode.

"Harper," I bit out, my voice rough.

She paused and drew back, the act itself almost making me lose the thin thread of control I was holding onto. Her eyes whipped up, dark blue through her lashes, which were damp and spiky from the rain. I meant to say something. Hell if I knew what. That brief pause helped me regain a smidgen of control. Before she set to licking, stroking and sucking me to the very edge of my sanity. My mind zeroed in on one thing—I wanted to be inside of her.

It was an act of pure will, driven by the lash of my need, to step back and pull her up roughly. Her lips were swollen and pink between our kisses and what she'd just been doing to my cock. I was beyond anything even resembling control. I shoved at her running pants, which were fitted as it was and damp on top of it. As a result, she almost fell over in the course of me nearly tearing them off. A half-wall ran a few feet alongside the door where a shelf held keys and the like that I tended to toss there when I entered.

In Harper's stumble, she caught her balance on the top of the wall and paused to kick her shoes off and free her legs from the tangle. Her bottom, that delectably lush bottom, faced me, and my last bit of restraint snapped. I stepped to her and ran a palm down her back, grimly savoring the hitch in her breath and the feel of her skin pebbling under my touch. I took another step, my cock brushing against her. Her back arched naturally as I dragged my palm in another pass along her spine, this time sliding down into the cleft between her thighs. I slid a finger through her folds, slicking it in her wetness. She was so wet, I almost came at the thought of how it would feel to sink inside of her. That flickering thought drove me, and I positioned myself behind her, gripping my cock in my hand and dragging it back and forth against her.

She moaned and arched further, her bottom rising to me. I was so far gone, I almost forgot a condom. At the last second, my cock in my fist and its tip resting at the entrance to her core, I remembered.

"Bloody hell! Hang on..."

I started to step away and whipped back to her when she spoke.

She was looking over her shoulder, the sight of her so sexy, it hit me right in the chest. With her damp locks partially drying, her hair was a rumpled mess. Her eyes were dark and her cheeks flushed. "Where are you going?" she asked, her question impatient, her tone husky.

I swallowed. "Condom."

She shook her head. "I'm on the pill. Until you, there was no one for four years. I'm not worried if you're not."

I stared at her. "Are you...?"

Her eyes darkened further. "Oh. My. God. If I wasn't sure, I wouldn't say anything."

She started to straighten, but that's all I needed. I was back behind her in a flash. I glanced down between us. Wetness slicked her folds, tempting me further even though I was already ruled by my need. My cock was about to burst, but I hung on with every ounce of control I had left and slowly eased inside of her. Her channel throbbed around me, its warm, wet, pulsing clench felt so bloody good, I groaned. I gripped her hip with one hand and slid the other up her back and threaded my fingers in her hair as I set to rocking into her.

She'd taken me so close to the edge before, I was there already, pleasure thundering through me with every drive into her. I hung on, determined she'd find her release first. I slipped my hand down through her curls, finding her clit hot, swollen and wet. She cried out, her creamy clench tightening around my cock and sending me hurtling. My release pounded through me and poured into her. I eased my grip on her hair and curled my hands over hers where she held onto the wall. We stood like that with me leaning over her, my forehead resting in the dip of her shoulder, breathing her scent in, as we slowly caught our breath.

After a few moments, I felt her skin pebbling again and realized she must be cold. Between running through the rain and the heat of our encounter dissipating, it figured she would be. I straightened and stepped back, regretfully sliding out of her, and lifted her into my arms.

She didn't resist and relaxed into my hold, her eyes flicking up to mine. "Where are we going?" she asked, a subtle smile curling one corner of her mouth.

"Shower."

Chapter Sixteen

HARPER

I stepped into the hallway outside Alex's front door, reluctant to leave. Although I didn't have to work today, I'd promised Olivia I'd stop by and help her paint the extra bedroom in the apartment she shared with Liam. They were in the midst of looking for a house to buy and sprucing up the apartment in advance. I looked up at Alex, straight into his dark chocolate gaze, and felt my heart thump. It should've been enough that we'd just ripped each other's clothes off and he'd sent me flying with another intense climax, but it wasn't. I hadn't allowed myself to give in to how much and how often I wanted him. I kept thinking I'd start to slake my need. The opposite seemed to be happening. Every time I was with him, the need gripped me more deeply. I was about to say something when I heard a sound.

I glanced to the main entrance door, which had been left slightly ajar. I surmised Alex and I hadn't quite closed it in our rushed stumble inside. Callie stepped through the door, a soft mewling sound coming from her. She was drenched. Her fur, a calico mix of brown, black and gold, was sticking up in spikes here and there and wet everywhere. Her mostly gold face lifted, her dark eyes looking at us. For a moment, we both froze. When she didn't dash away, I knelt down.

"Hey Callie girl," I said, trying to keep my voice low.

Alex stepped into the hallway and knelt beside me. He was quiet and simply held a hand out. Callie approached slowly, while I hardly dared to breathe. She looked rather bedraggled and was likely cold. I glanced through the window outside to see the rain had picked up from its earlier drizzle and was falling steadily now. She incrementally approached us, sidling along the hallway wall until she reached Alex. After a moment of complete stillness, she sniffed his hand and remained still when he softly scratched under her chin. She emitted a rumbling purr.

I looked at him and was torn between laughter and tears, although I kept my emotions in check. Here was this man, tall, strong and imposing, called the Beast by his teammates, trying to make himself as reassuring as possible for a stray cat. I didn't know what to think of what it said about him as a man. Perhaps, it was more honest to say I didn't know what to think of what he was coming to mean to me. As a man, he held true strength, the kind where he didn't need to use it to intimidate anyone. Underneath his thoroughly masculine, alpha-sexy exterior beat the heart of a true gentleman and a softie to boot.

I thought Callie was precious, but she looked rather pathetic at the moment. She was wet, dirty and skinny. After a few quiet moments of Alex rubbing her chin, she dashed past him into his apartment. He stood slowly and glanced to me, his eyes questioning. I gestured with my hand for him to close the door, so he did.

"Do you have food for her?" I whispered, hoping the sound of my voice wouldn't scare Callie.

"No. I didn't... Dammit. I didn't even

think of that. What else do I need?" he asked in whisper.

"I thought you'd been leaving food out for her."

"Just things like leftover chicken and tuna," he said with a shrug.

"Have you ever had a cat?"

He shook his head, his eyes wide and worried.

I bit my lip to keep from laughing aloud. "Okay, you need food, a litter box and cat litter. How about I go get everything and you stay here?"

He nodded quickly. I started to turn away and then spun back. "Maybe let her explore a bit, but if it looks like she's getting skittish, open the door. We don't want her to feel trapped. She's been living under the stairs here long enough, I doubt she'll take off."

I started to turn away again when I felt his hand curl around my arm. He reeled me back, right into his arms. "Thanks," he said gruffly before dipping his head for a kiss.

All he did was brush his lips against mine, but it felt so damn good, it left me flustered. I watched as he stepped away and quietly went back into his apartment. I jogged the few blocks back to my place and quickly changed into dry clothes before heading out to the grocery store.

I called Olivia on the way.

"Hey, what's up?" she asked as soon as she picked up.

"Just calling to let you know I might be a little later than I planned."

"Okay. If you don't have time…"

"Oh no. I have time. I'm just picking up cat supplies for Alex."

"Now you have to explain," she said, and I could hear the smile in her voice.

I quickly summarized how he'd been trying to lure Callie inside and Callie finally braving the inside this morning. Olivia laughed, the sound petering out with a sigh.

"You know, I've been trying to stay out of your way, but Alex is a really great guy. In case you hadn't noticed yet," she said pointedly.

I took a breath and tried to beat back the little dance my heart did. "I've noticed," I finally said.

My chest tightened and a funny feeling rose inside. It was so unfamiliar, I wanted to shy away, but it was like a ray of sun casting a beam across my heart and I couldn't ignore it. It was joy. Something I'd thought long gone from my life. I'd been content with feeling peaceful and not afraid. I hadn't dared to consider more. Most certainly not what I felt with Alex—this scalding hot desire, softened only by the way it felt to be with him. He was so strong, so protective, that I wanted nothing other than to wrap myself in him. Safe wasn't something I'd ever counted on again, but it's how I felt with Alex...and *that* scared the hell out of me.

"While I'm at it, I also think Daisy's right. You're not really a fling kind of person," Olivia added.

Laughter bubbled up. My emotions were running so high, I felt almost punch drunk. When I could catch my breath, I said, "Wow, Daisy would love to hear you think she's right."

"I'll make sure to tell her. Meanwhile, nice deflection there. No comment on whether you're a fling person?" she asked.

I bit my lip and clicked on my blinker to turn into the grocery store parking lot. "Maybe I'm not. I'll have to think about it."

"Well, while you're thinking about it, don't forget there aren't too many guys who would play the long game to take care of a stray cat. Alex is one of a rare few. Plus, he's totally hot. Not my kind of hot, but you're kind. And he's way into you." I could hear another voice in the background. "Gotta go. Liam's about to fall off the ladder. I'll see you whenever you get here."

———

A few hours later, I stood in the hallway outside Alex's door again. Callie was still inside. She'd gone outside once or twice while he'd wisely opened the backdoor of his apartment, which opened onto a small, enclosed yard. She'd carefully investigated the yard and leapt the fence to run around the front and check her little spot under the stairs. The rain kept falling all day. After her brief return to the outside, she'd raced back inside and curled up on the windowsill on a small pillow Alex had placed there for her when she kept circling and trying to get comfortable.

I could've stayed there all day and *really* wanted to, yet the depth of that wanting made me anxious, so I found myself where I was. Looking up at Alex, rubbing the soft fabric of my sweatshirt hem between my fingers and clutching my car keys with the other. "Well, I should go. Olivia's probably wondering where I am now."

His dark eyes held mine. After a beat, he

nodded. "Right then. I'd offer to come with you, but..." He gestured behind him.

"You have to stay with Callie," I said quickly.

"How about you come back later? You could bring Stanley back with you," he offered with a slight smile.

I had brought Stanley with me after my trip to the store. He'd wandered in the back yard and curled up by the door. Callie didn't seem bothered by him, and Stanley had enough sense to hang back. At the moment, Stanley was waiting by the outer door, his eyes pinned to the street. Before I thought about it, I was nodding. Because that's exactly what I wanted to do. Come back here and curl up on Alex's couch while it was raining.

At my nod, Alex flashed another one of his devastating grins. His grins weren't thrown around casually, so every time I got one, my heart did a little hop, skip and jump. He dipped his head and brushed his lips across mine. I instinctively flexed into him.

"Not enough," I murmured against his lips as I slipped my hand into his rumpled hair and tugged him to me.

I could feel his smile against my lips, just before his tongue swept into my mouth. He lifted me against him and spun me against the door behind us. I'd gotten more than I bargained for with his hard, hot body pressed against mine. There were kisses and then there were Alex's kisses—long, slow, hot, and deep. By the time I came up for air, it was a damn good thing I had the wall behind me and Alex holding me up. Otherwise, I'd have melted to the floor. Somehow I managed to gather myself together enough to push away from the wall when Alex stepped back.

"Okay, then...I'll see you later," I said weakly, little shocks of pleasure pinging through my body.

He reached over and brushed a lock of hair off my cheek, tucking it behind my ear. A shiver chased in the wake of his touch. "Okay then."

I had to order my feet to move and made my way down his front steps on shaky legs. I reached the sidewalk and stopped, discombobulated enough I couldn't recall where my car was. Stanley nudged my leg and I glanced down to see him looking to the right. Following his gaze, I remembered where my car was—a block down the street on the other side. I gave myself a mental shake and started walking that way, Stanley following alongside me, his presence steady and calm.

We crossed the street. I had my keys in hand and my eyes on my car when I heard a voice call my name. I reflexively turned toward the voice, but my body reacted before I knew for certain who it was. Dread coiled in the pit of my stomach, a flash of panic knotting my chest. I didn't want to look, but my eyes went right to Joe Schmidt. He stood a short distance beyond my car. He was tall and lanky. His dull blonde hair was damp from the rain. I swallowed and fought the urge to run. I was frozen in place, my feet rooted to the sidewalk. Stanley stepped closer to me, his body pressing against my leg. I could feel his low growl rumbling.

I stared at Joe, unable to look away. He looked back at me, his flat gray eyes exactly as I remembered. I'd only seen him a few times up close, but the expression in his eyes had been the same—flat with a hint of anger. I didn't remember the look in his eyes when he raped me. I watched as Joe closed the distance between us, panic tightening like a vise around my throat and chest. He stopped a few feet away, as if conscious of the fact we were on the street in full view of anyone who happened to be nearby.

"Tell your boyfriend to back off," Joe said, his expression never changing. "I don't have anything else to answer for and I sure as hell don't need the media stirring this shit up."

I stared at him, genuinely puzzled by what he meant. Alex hadn't done anything with the press. In fact, I'd said more to the press with my interview than Alex had at all. Anger rose inside, a forceful wave rocking me. I could feel myself shaking, tremors rippling through me. This feeling—the fear, the panic, the inability to reel in my visceral reaction to Joe—had been what drove me to accept the prosecutor's suggestion that they offer a plea deal to Joe. I had the option to refuse, but the months of volleys from his defense attorney had only made it worse. I'd gone from numb to paralyzed by anxiety and so many sleepless nights, I could hardly function. It had been a relief when it all ended.

I finally managed to speak. "You got off easy, and you damn well know it," I spat out, experiencing a flash of satisfaction when Joe's eyes widened slightly. I imagined he thought his intimidation tactics would work with me. He should've remembered I'd fought like hell before even if I didn't have enough strength and force to hold him off. "Alex hasn't talked to the press, but I have and I'll keep doing it if I feel like it. You took the deal they offered and it didn't involve me keeping my mouth shut."

"You fuckin' bitch," Joe said, advancing on me.

Panic roared through me—I felt cold and numb all over, my hands tingly and my pulse racing so fast, I could hardly breathe. I heard my name again. This time it was Alex's voice, the sound of it ringing like a bell inside of me. Relief hit me so hard, I almost stumbled. Before I could even turn to see him approaching, I heard someone call his name. I turned to see Alex running toward Joe with Ethan hot on his heels. Alex bolted past me, his hand curling into Joe's jacket and yanking him off his feet.

Ethan caught Alex's arm just as he pulled it back, I assumed to plow it into Joe's sneering face. Alex tried to shake free, but Ethan didn't back down. "Don't make things worse, mate."

Alex never even turned Ethan's way and held tight to Joe. "Back the fuck off, you bloody arse. Don't you dare come near her again. Understood?"

Spit flew from Alex's mouth and landed on Joe's face, the force of his words vibrating with his anger. Ethan caught my eyes and nodded his head toward Alex's building. I had no idea where he'd come from. I'm sure Alex would've preferred I get the hell out of the way, but I wasn't going anywhere.

Ethan's focus shifted away from me when Alex tried to shake his arm free again. Ethan held firm. "Bloody hell," Alex muttered. He eased his grip on Joe's shirt and took a step back. "Stay the hell away from her."

Joe's sneer hadn't faded. "Not gonna look too good for you now, is it?" he taunted.

Ethan stepped in front of Alex, literally shoving him out of the way. It was only now dawning on me Joe might've been trying to provoke Alex. Ethan's unexpected appearance was a huge relief, if only because he had the height and strength to contain Alex. While a part of me would've relished witnessing Joe get his ass kicked, I didn't want Alex in any more legal trouble than he already was.

"You got nowhere with this," Ethan snarled, his finger in Joe's face. "Now get the fuck out of here before I punch you next."

Joe backed away rapidly. "Fuck off!" he called as he reached the corner and bolted down a side street.

Ethan turned back to us, his gaze scanning Alex. "Don't follow him, mate. That's what he wants."

Alex glared at him. "What the hell are you doing here?"

"Saving your bloody arse from more charges," Ethan retorted.

Joe was out of sight now. Alex's fists were clenched and his features hard. After a moment, he gave his head a shake and looked to me, his concerned gaze coasting over me. "Are you okay? What did he say to you?"

"Not much. He said to tell you to back off and something about not needing the media to stir things up." My entire body was buzzing—the panicky numbness had given way to relief.

Alex stepped to my side, his palm sliding down my back in a slow pass. His touch was so comforting and his presence so strong, I wanted to collapse against him.

"Hey, easy luv. You're shaking. Fuck, are you sure you're okay? That fucking asshole. I'll..."

Alex had started to tense up, and I shook my head. "You will not chase after him," I managed. I hadn't even noticed I was still shaking, but my brain was functioning enough to know Ethan was right. It was way too convenient that Joe happened to be across the street from Alex's apartment and happened to be there right after I was leaving. The thought that he might've been watching us sent a cold bolt of fear through me. "I'm fine. The shaking thing is just because...well, just because. Come on, let's go inside."

Ethan walked in silence beside us as we crossed the street and returned to Alex's apartment. Stanley was pretty much glued to my side, his solid, steady presence warm and comforting. I'd completely lost track of the fact it was still raining until we stepped back into Alex's apartment. He strode quickly to the bathroom and returned with a towel as I sank into one of the chairs at his kitchen table. Ethan shook his jacket off and hung it by the door before sitting down with me.

He glanced over at Alex who stood by the counter, his hands gripping the edge of it as he looked over at me. I didn't know how to interpret what was held in his gaze. It was dark and intent. Meanwhile, I was still reverberating internally from being closer to Joe than I'd been since he raped me. I'd had to see him in court a few times, but it had always been at a distance and the entire setting around us completely controlled. The times I'd seen him in the park had also been enough of a distance I hadn't really felt what it was like to be near him.

Ethan's voice made me jump. "Thought I'd stop by to check on your cat," he said with a shrug. "Good thing, eh?"

Alex looked to him, his gaze puzzled. "Huh?"

Ethan drummed his fingers on the table. "Liam said you've got some stray. I was driving by, so figured I'd come see for myself. You're such a softie." He flashed a sly grin, and I sensed he was doing his damnedest to snap Alex out of his thoughts.

All things considered, I figured that might be a good thing right now. I didn't want to dwell on what just happened and certainly not now. Alex's gaze cleared, and he glanced to the window. Callie was still there, curled up on the little cushion. For a stray, she had an endearing preference for soft places to sleep. "Aye. There she is. How does Liam know? She just finally came inside this morning," he said, glancing back to Ethan.

Ethan looked over at Callie. "She's a scraggly little thing, eh?" He glanced back to Alex. "I dunno how Liam knew. He just did."

"I told Olivia when I called to tell her I'd be later than I planned," I said, suddenly recalling I had been on my way to see her before "Oh, I have to go!"

I stood abruptly. Alex immediately pushed away from the counter. "Don't go."

My heart gave a squeeze, and I wanted, oh how I wanted, to just stay right here in the haven of him. Oddly, I pushed back against that feeling. I'd spent so much time putting the pieces of myself back together, I didn't want to let myself stumble back to a place where I worried about Joe and if I might encounter him somewhere. Even though I had plenty of misgivings about seeing him and plenty more about how it seemed he'd tried to up the ante on Alex's charges, I couldn't let him cow me. I shook my head. "It's okay. I told Olivia I'd be over this afternoon, and I will. I'm not letting this change what I was planning to do."

His gaze held mine, the force of it intense. His shoulders rose and fell with a deep breath. "Please stay," he repeated.

I stepped to him and put my palm on his chest. His heart beat strong and steady underneath my touch. "I need to do this. Okay?"

Another deep breath, and he closed his eyes. When he opened them again, his expression was pained, but he managed a nod. "Okay. I'll walk you to your car."

Ethan stood with us and called to Alex

when we reached the door. "Don't forget we've got practice in an hour. We can ride over together if you want."

Alex glanced back, looking startled, his expression clearing after a second. "Bloody hell. Forgetting everything today. Sit tight, and I'll be right back," he said to Ethan.

Ethan nodded, his eyes catching mine. "We've got your back, Harper. You know that, right?"

Warmth bloomed in my chest. Ethan's usual teasing manner had disappeared, and I was beyond relieved he'd chanced to stop by Alex's place today. He'd kept a bad situation from getting far worse, and I figured his presence with Alex now would keep him from dwelling on Joe. I nodded. "I know. Hey, do me a favor?"

"Anything," he said quickly.

"Keep Alex out of trouble."

Ethan flashed a grin. "As long as I'm around, I'll do my best."

ALEX

I threw myself into practice and was relieved Coach put us through a grueling one today. He started us off with running drills and didn't let up for two full hours. We had a big game coming up in two weeks against a team we'd lost to last season. So far this year, we were ranked first in our conference and we wanted to keep it that way. After practice, I raced through a shower. The moment my focus from play ended, my mind spun right back to Harper. She was the wind that spun my weathervane, always spinning in reflex toward her. Ethan was conveniently as quick as I was and met me at the locker room doors. We stepped into the hallway together.

"Think maybe we should tell Coach what happened," he said.

"Bloody hell," I muttered in reply. "Nothing happened. You kept me from beating the guy senseless, so there's no story."

I was still disgruntled about that. I had enough brains to know it was probably for the best Ethan had chanced to stop by my flat, but damn I wanted to bash Joe's face in. Every time I thought of the way Harper had looked when I saw her from my window, my gut churned and anger rolled through me. Even from a distance, I could tell she'd frozen. I'd only been watching her because, well, she'd just left and I'd already been wishing she was back. I hadn't even seen Joe when I knew something was wrong. It wasn't until I ran out the front entrance that I saw him. I'd gone from worried about her to boiling mad at him inside of a second.

Ethan stopped walking. We were alone in the long stadium hallway at the moment. Voices from the locker room carried in soft echoes toward us. I paused mid-stride and glanced to him. "What?"

"If you think that asshole won't be mentioning that little encounter, you've gone bloody stupid on me," he said with a shake of his head. "Head this off, so Coach can get out in front of it. That's all I'm saying."

Ethan, so similar to Liam in some ways, could trick you into thinking he was shallow. He liked to tease and flirt and play the joker. It served him well on the pitch. He was a ferocious defender. For players who hadn't had the experience of facing him in play, he often held the upper hand by virtue of the fact he gave off a casual, couldn't be bothered air. He hid an intense focus and ruthless skill behind his laissez faire manner. He was a damn good mate too. I knew he'd likely wanted to let me pound Joe, but he'd known it would only bring me more trouble. I didn't like to admit it, but I knew he was right about talking to Coach.

I nodded. "Fine. Let's do this then."

We commenced to walking again, stopping at the door to Coach's office. It was closed, and we could hear the low murmur of voices. I glanced to Ethan and arched a brow in question. He shrugged and knocked on the door.

"Come in," Coach called.

We opened the door to find Zoe seated across from Coach. I was mentally prepared to talk with Coach, but I wasn't so sure I was ready to fill my attorney in because my guess was Zoe would think I'd been stupid. Nothing to do about it though. She was here.

She stood up from her chair, turning to face Ethan and me. "Alex, good to see you." Her eyes flicked to Ethan.

I opened my mouth to introduce them, but Ethan beat me to it. He flashed a roguish grin, his green eyes crinkling at the corners. "Hello there. Ethan Walsh," he said, stepping to Zoe, a tad closer than he should, but that's what Ethan did when it came to beautiful women. There was not even a spark for me with Zoe, but it didn't mean I didn't notice she was gorgeous. With her auburn hair, hazel eyes and long legs, she was impossible not to notice. She shook Ethan's hand, her eyes holding his. He winked and a subtle flush crested her cheeks. Well, well. Maybe Ethan could crack her composure.

She shook his hand briskly. "Zoe Lawson. I'm Alex's defense attorney."

Ethan glanced from her to me as she stepped back from him. "Ah. Perfect then. I dragged our good boy here because I figured he needed to fill Coach in on something. Even better to have you here."

Bloody hell. Why did Ethan have to be so forward? It's not that I planned to hide what happened from Zoe, but I'd have preferred to run it by Coach first.

Coach looked between us and gestured for us to sit. "Have a seat and fill us in."

There were three chairs opposite Coach's desk. Ethan quickly slipped into the one beside Zoe. All eyes turned to me as I sat down next to him. I sighed and ran a hand through my damp hair. "It was nothing when all was said and done."

Zoe circled her hand, gesturing for me to continue. "Carry on."

"Harper was leaving my flat, and Joe was on the sidewalk. I almost hit him again, but I didn't," I finally said.

Coach arched a brow and looked to Ethan.

Ethan rolled his eyes at me before answering. "He might've missed a few details. I'd stopped by his place and saw him bolting across the street. I didn't know who he was after, but I know what Alex looks like when he's pissed, so I chased after him. He got up in Joe's face, and I had to keep a lock on his arm to keep him from being stupid again. He backed off, and that was that. If you ask me, I think Joe wasn't there by accident. I can't say he knew he'd luck into pissing Alex off again, but it bloody hell felt like he was looking for a fight."

Zoe drummed her fingers on the arm of her chair, her eyes flicking from Ethan to me. She was quiet though and glanced to Coach who shook his head and sighed.

"Alex, you can thank Ethan for helping you scoot past that little problem. We don't need you facing more charges," Coach said before looking to Zoe.

She nodded firmly. "Exactly my sentiments. However, since you managed to not make this worse, I'll be in touch with the prosecutor about this. It's not good to have Mr. Schmidt hanging around where you live and definitely won't look good that he was around Harper. Did he say anything to her?"

"She said he told her to tell me to back off. Look, I get I need to keep my nose clean. It's not like I run around punching guys all the time. But this is bullshit. If he shows up around her again, I... Hell, I don't know if it's stupid to hit him or not. The man *raped* her. I mean, bloody hell! What the fuck is he doing anywhere near her? I don't..." I bit back my words and leaned my head into my hands, trying to gather myself. Every time I thought about what Joe did to Harper, I wanted to spit nails.

"It's definitely bullshit," Ethan said, his tone somber and tinged with anger.

I ran my hands through my hair before straightening and glancing to him. I swallowed against the anger knotted in my chest and took a slow breath. It helped knowing I wasn't crazy to feel how I did, but I felt so bloody helpless. When Joe wasn't right in front of me, I knew perfectly well it wouldn't do a damn bit of good for Harper for me to pound the hell out of him. I didn't particularly care for my own consequences for that. I wanted to roll back time and have him tossed in the slammer for years over what he did to her.

Zoe caught my eyes. "I'll have a chat with the prosecutor. He knows it won't help Joe for it to look like he's hanging around the woman he attacked. No matter what he says about the rape charges, he pled guilty to assault charges against her. Even though the current charges are against you, juries don't like to side with unsympathetic victims. He didn't look good before and this will make it worse."

She smoothed her skirt and stood. I noticed Ethan's eyes travel down her long legs and back up and almost laughed. If anything could lighten my mood, Ethan looking gobsmacked might do it. I expected him to toss a sly grin her way, but he didn't. He tore his gaze free and stared at the floor, the hint of a flush on his cheeks. Well, well. Perhaps my uptight, kick-ass defense attorney might crack Ethan's composure. I'd pay money to see that.

Zoe looked to Coach and then to me before nodding firmly as she adjusted the strap of her purse over her shoulder. "I'll follow up after I've spoken to the prosecutor."

"Wait a minute. Did you have another update?" I asked, realizing we'd only discussed my little run in with Joe this afternoon.

"Oh right. I was in the area and dropped by to let you guys know the prosecutor was open to lesser charges. Mr. Schmidt isn't too fond of the attention to his past and would like this to go away sooner rather than later. I didn't agree to anything and now I'll be heading back to talk with him." Her eyes narrowed as she held my gaze. "If you see Mr. Schmidt again, walk in the opposite direction. Understood?"

I nodded, but I didn't say aloud that if Joe happened to be anywhere near Harper, I wasn't making any promises about what I might do.

Zoe left, just as Coach's phone rang, and

he shooed us out. As Ethan and I walked down the hallway, his eyes were pinned to Zoe who was a bit ahead of us. Even her walk was no-nonsense, her low-heeled boots striking the floor with precision. I glanced sideways at him. "Don't forget to blink, mate."

Ethan's gaze whipped to mine, and he cracked a wry grin. "You must admit your attorney's bloody gorgeous."

I shrugged, mostly to annoy him. His eyes narrowed. "Mate, you're not blind."

"Obviously not. She's pretty, but not my type. Clearly, she's yours. Think she might be a bit out of your league though."

Ethan glared at me. "Bloody hell, she's not."

"I don't mean in looks. You've plenty of women drooling over you, but she's smart. Really smart. Honestly, she almost scares me. I get the impression she raises a ruckus in court to win her cases. I'm damn pleased she's on my side, I'll say that much."

Ethan flashed another sly grin. "Right? She's brilliant and beautiful. She's so buttoned up, I'd like to see her lose control."

I shook my head. "Mate, don't piss her off until this mess with me is cleared up."

He chuckled as we pushed through the

doorway outside. "Aye. I'd never piss a lady off."

I merely shook my head.

He flashed another grin and nodded. "Right then. Okay, let's get you home. I'll walk you to your door so you don't hit anyone on the way in."

I elbowed him and followed him to his car, Ethan laughing every step of the way.

I watched the paint roll onto the wall under the roller I held. There was something so soothing and satisfying about painting. It could make a room an entirely different space. It painted away old marks and scars on the wall, leaving a fresh, clean surface behind. I hadn't planned it this way, but it couldn't have been a better activity for me after the day's events. It was only three o'clock, yet my day had been chock full of emotional intensity to the point I felt punch-drunk from it all. The sex with Alex had been, well, amazing, mind-blowing, earth shattering and so intimate it made me blush just thinking about it. Being taken from behind like that in the way only Alex could be rough and gentle at once had left me breathless and reeling. A steaming shower where I got to enjoy the mouth-watering sight of Alex's rock hard body slicked with soap had been another little gift of the morning.

To encounter Joe on the heels of that had been like a pendulum swinging so hard and fast inside, it sent me flying against a wall and falling to the ground in bewilderment. I paused and dipped my roller in the paint tray. Olivia had selected a soft gray for this room. Her landlord had offered her and Liam two months rent-free if they painted the whole apartment before they moved out. It's not like they needed to save the money, but they were all over it. Olivia had opted for neutral tones for the entire apartment. They were down to this guest bedroom and the kitchen.

"So, did you want to talk about today?" Olivia asked, her voice lilting above the steady sound of the paint rollers on the wall.

I knew Liam had heard about the encounter with Joe and had called Olivia. She hadn't said much, but had enveloped me in a hug when I arrived. She was good about waiting to talk. I couldn't say the same for Daisy, but then Daisy was the perfect antidote to being stuck on something. I kept watching the paint roll on the wall, considering whether I wanted to talk. Oddly enough, I did. But not about Joe.

"I don't know what to do about Alex," I finally said, pausing again to dip the roller into the paint tray.

Olivia was painting the wall opposite me and glanced over her shoulder, a furrow appearing between her brows. "You want to talk about Alex?"

I straightened and commenced to roll more paint on the wall as I moved to the lower section. "I suppose you think I might want to talk about seeing Joe. Funny thing is all this stuff getting stirred up around him has been good. I mean, it sucks to see him. I'd be happy if he moved to another planet and I never had to see him again. But, it's ended up being good because I'm doing okay. Don't get me wrong, I freak out inside, but then I bounce back."

I glanced over my shoulder to see Olivia had stopped painting, the roller in her hand pressed against the wall and paint starting to run in drips below it. "Hey, keep moving," I said, gesturing with my elbow to the wall.

"Oh, right," she said, turning back and starting to paint again. "Well, I guess that's good then. Weird, but good. Wait, I didn't mean to say it was weird..."

"It's okay. I think it's weird too, but whatever," I interjected.

"So Alex then. I'd much rather talk about Alex anyway," she offered with a soft laugh. "What do you mean you don't know what to do?"

"Um, just that," I replied, feeling my cheeks heat a little. This whole Alex thing was uncomfortable on so many levels. I'd been a bit relieved, to be honest, to figure relationships just weren't my thing after what happened. The drama, the uncertainty, all of that was something I thought I'd get to escape. Then along came Alex. One kiss nearly melted me. My silly fling idea was looking sillier by the day. Even worse, my past experiences with relationships hadn't prepared me for the feelings Alex elicited—this intense need to connect, a seemingly insatiable longing for him, and an intimacy that knitted us tighter and tighter together every time I was with him.

I heard nothing but the sound of paint rollers moving in unison for a few beats and started to wonder if Olivia was going to reply and got anxious about it. I felt so silly and ridiculous. Daisy had presciently tried to point out that my whole idea of a fling didn't quite suit my personality, but I'd dismissed her. I'd been too caught up in the chance to bolt past my buried fears about having sex. With anyone. Ever again.

"Okay, I'm going to be blunt here. It's obvious you like Alex. A lot. I thought you were crazy to jump into bed with him because it just wasn't like you. The only reason I didn't get all protective about it was because I know what a good guy Alex is. He wouldn't hurt a fly." She stopped to dip her roller in the paint tray and glanced to me. "Okay, well, he punched Joe but Joe deserved a lot worse."

She straightened and resumed painting. "It's also obvious Alex likes you. A lot, a lot. Liam's convinced Alex is done for when it comes to you."

"Done for?"

"He thinks Alex's in love and that's it. Alex is super loyal to his friends and family. According to Liam, he sends money back to his mum to take care of her and paid for both of his sisters to go to college. He's that kind of guy. And now Liam thinks you're Alex's girl. Liam's known Alex since they were kids. If he thinks you're it for Alex, I'm inclined to think he's right." She glanced over her shoulder and nodded toward my paint roller.

I looked over to see I'd stopped painting and drips were almost to the bottom of the wall. "Dammit!" I swiftly rolled over the drips and set the roller down. I didn't quite know how to absorb the idea I might mean that much to Alex. Part of me wanted to jump for joy, yet it was also half-terrifying.

The paint tray needed a refill, so I stepped to the corner where we'd left the can of paint and carried it over. While I added paint to the tray, Olivia continued talking.

"So if you're asking what to do about Alex, I think you need to think about what you want. It's not fair to him to keep this going if you don't mean for it to go anywhere. But I don't think you feel that way. I guess it comes down to whether you're ready for this or not."

I set the paint can back in the corner, dipped the roller in the paint and resumed painting. "Ready for what?" I asked, anxiety spinning in my chest.

Olivia didn't even try to hide her sigh. "Okay, you kept me from losing my mind over Liam, so I guess it's my turn. Ready for something serious with Alex. That's what I meant and you know it."

I was painting so fast now the roller zoomed off the wall and into my leg. I paused and tried to take a breath and slow my heart rate. I turned to face her, watching the paint roll in smooth passes on the wall as she painted.

"Okay, okay. So how do I know if it's the right thing?"

I asked the question, but I already knew the answer. Alex had blown through my defenses, knocking them down as if they were cardboard cutouts. It hadn't been much more than a month since I'd encountered him in the park and been crazy enough to kiss him. Now, every night I didn't have with him, I missed him. I was shadowboxing—with my past and the dreams I'd forced myself to give up. It was hard to let myself be vulnerable. I didn't like it.

Olivia hadn't answered my question, but she stopped painting and turned to face me, her green gaze coasting over me. After a beat, she spoke. "I think you already know. You just have to decide if you want it."

Tears pressed at the back of my eyes and emotion clogged my throat. That emotional messiness I thought I'd gotten a pass from? Not so much. My emotions were crashing through me in waves and threatening to catch me in a riptide.

Olivia stepped to me and pulled me into a hug. "No matter what, you'll be fine," she said as she stepped back. "You're one of the strongest people I know and don't ever forget it."

I looked down and realized I'd never set my paint roller down. We had matching blotches of paint on our legs now. We started to laugh simultaneously. After we caught our breath, she looked over at me. "Well?"

"I'll keep you posted."

"Okay, let's finish this room and get cleaned up. Wanna stay for dinner after we're done?" she asked.

I felt the grin tugging at the corners of my mouth. "Can't. I told Alex I'd be over later."

Olivia grinned. "Ah, I see. Might I point out again the list of men who take in stray cats is very short?"

Chapter Nineteen

ALEX

I leaned back in my chair, carefully keeping my emotions in check. Zoe had dragged me down for a meeting with the prosecutor. I didn't want to be here, my sentiments exacerbated by the arrogant prosecutor. Brian Wheeler, the prosecutor in question, sat across from Zoe and me in his office. The hum of noise from the hallway filtered through the door. The Seattle District Attorney's offices were a hubbub of commotion. Brian looked up from the document he'd been reviewing and glanced from Zoe to me, his dark gaze inscrutable. I was accustomed to players from opposing teams trying to do what Brian seemed to be after—intimidation. On the pitch, it never got to me. If anything, other players trying to rile me up only sank me deeper into my focus when I tuned them out. Yet, here with him, I had to try to think about anything other than why we were here. Otherwise, I was angry. The whole bloody situation pissed me off. Joe should've never been given the chance to walk away from what he did to Harper with what amounted to a light slap on the wrist.

Sure, I hit Joe. Hell, I'd do it again if he got anywhere near Harper. It didn't change history though, nor did it amount to anything remotely close to what he'd done to her. But, I kept my cool. I called on years of discipline and kept my expression blank. Brian finally looked away from me and back to Zoe.

"I'll need to talk with Mr. Schmidt, but I'm inclined to think he'll accept this," Brian said before looking back to me. "If he does, you can count yourself lucky here. The charge for assault could easily hold up in court."

Before I had a chance to reply, Zoe spoke. "I wouldn't be so confident, Brian. Mr. Schmidt is not a sympathetic figure as I'm sure you're aware. Before we agree to anything, I'd also like to discuss my concerns about Mr. Schmidt showing up outside my client's apartment and approaching Ms. Jacobs on the street. It appears he was trying to provoke her and perhaps my client, neither of which is acceptable."

Brian's eyes gave nothing away, but lines of tension bracketed his mouth. "Your concerns are noted. I realize this might be difficult for you to believe, but it's possible Mr. Schmidt happened to be there by chance. He does live in the area."

Zoe's expression stayed calm, but I sensed the steel underneath. "If it happens again, I'll bring it up with the judge."

Brian didn't reply and merely nodded. A few minutes later, I'd followed Zoe out to a waiting room. She was sitting beside me, quietly checking emails on her phone while I wondered when the hell we could leave, when someone said her name. Zoe glanced up and actually smiled. I almost chuckled aloud because I realized Ethan would love to see her smile. Her usually tense face softened, and her gaze, always serious when I'd seen her, brightened. "Hey Becca! How's it going?"

I followed her eyes to a woman approaching from the hallway. She was tall with glossy dark hair pulled back in a bun and bright blue eyes. Another beautiful woman who elicited absolutely nothing from me.

Harper had ruined other women me, and I needed to face it.

The woman stopped in front of us. "Hey Zoe. I'd ask what brings you here, but Brian mentioned he was reviewing a proposed plea on that case. It's a damn good thing Mr. Schmidt wasn't assigned to me because I wouldn't have even wanted to give the jerk the time of day," she said with a shake of her head.

Zoe laughed softly and rolled her eyes. "Exactly why you didn't get his case. Becca, this is Alex Gordon." She caught my eyes and gestured between us. "Alex, this is Becca Mc-Namara. She's another prosecutor here. She mostly handles domestic violence and sexual assault cases."

I started to stand, but Becca shook her head. "Goodness, no need to stand. Nice to meet you. I'll have to tell my husband we met. He's a fan," she said with a grin.

I inclined my head with a nod. "Nice to meet you as well. Send your husband my best."

Becca glanced back at Zoe. "So what's the status?"

Zoe shrugged. "Brian doesn't like my offer, but I'm guessing he'll talk Mr. Schmidt into it. Good ol' Schmidt showed up outside

Alex's apartment and approached Ms. Jacobs. Doesn't look too sympathetic for a jury if we went to trial."

Becaa shook her head. "Definitely not. You know, I wish I'd been the prosecutor for Schmidt's old case. I was here then, but it went to someone else. I didn't think they should've offered a plea deal, but they did." She looked to me. "I probably shouldn't say this, but what the hell? Don't blame you."

Zoe let out a laugh and glanced to me. "See, told you people would think you were the hero."

I decided staying quiet was my best choice, so I simply nodded. Becca and Zoe moved onto another topic and a few minutes later Becca hurried away to take a call. Brian called Zoe back in a few minutes later, leaving me to wait. Fine with me. I just wanted this mess resolved.

Not much later, Zoe came striding back into the waiting room, stopping in front of me. "Looks like we have a deal. There'll be an administrative hearing later this week. You'll need to be available, and if you have to skip practice to be there, you'd better be there. If the judge approves, you'll plead to a lesser charge and agree to community service. Assuming you keep your nose clean for a full year after that, the charges will be removed from your record." She paused and narrowed her eyes. "Even if plenty of people understand why you're pissed at Mr. Schmidt, turn around and walk the other way if you ever see him. According to your Coach, you have the slowest fuse on his entire team. Love apparently makes you crazy, so don't be stupid again. Now come on, let's go," she said, turning and walking quickly out of the building as I followed.

After Zoe drove away, I stood on the sidewalk watching the cars roll by. I wanted to go see Harper, but I was holding back. She'd spent another night with me after our run-in with Joe. We were now halfway through the next week, and I'd only seen her when we went running in the mornings. I was coming to recognize that I'd better keep a grip on my sanity when it came to her. While I might have known what I wanted, it was becoming clear she wasn't on the same page yet. As long as we were skin to skin, the unspoken feelings and doubts crowding the space between us fell away. When we fell asleep together, I never wanted morning to come because I was starting to see the pattern. With the light of day, Harper kept herself back. Those old invisible walls I used to sense weren't reinforced the way they'd once been, but they were there. She hid behind them. Brutal understanding helped me recognize why they were there, but it didn't change what I wanted and knew we could have. If only she'd let me in for more than temporary passes.

I gave a mental shake, stuffed my hands in my pockets and started walking home. The sky was overcast, but it wasn't raining. Suited my mood to a tee. As I walked, the wheels in my mind spun over whether I should take a step back, or push a little harder with Harper.

Chapter Twenty

HARPER

My office phone rang and I hit the speaker button. "Yes?"

"Harper, it's Brad Williams from the Seattle Observer. How are you?"

I'd been in the middle of entering updates on a few patients in our electronic records system. With my brain in a different gear entirely, it took me a minute to absorb what Brad said. As soon as I did, I stopped typing and spun to face the phone, anxiety knotting in my chest. Brad had been nothing but respectful in his article about Joe's new charges. He'd adhered to our agreement that I be allowed to review everything before it was published. While I didn't like any of this and would rather erase the entire history of it, part of me was relieved to have it rehashed in the press. Back when it happened, I was too wrecked to pay much attention other than the fact I wanted it over—the trial and anything that reminded me of what happened. Brad's article not only touched on Alex's charges, but he reviewed some stats on just how thoroughly Joe had skated by when it came to my case. It was validating to see the truth of it in black and white with nothing but numbers to tell the story.

Yet, I had no idea why Brad was calling me again. The fact he was made me nervous. Because I didn't think he was calling just to say hi.

I cleared my throat. "Hi Brad. I'm okay. You?"

"Can't complain. Listen, I'm calling to follow up on the plea deal agreed upon at Mr. Gordon's hearing yesterday. I have a few questions. Do you mind?"

My stomach churned. I'd been avoiding asking Alex about this very issue. Truth was, I was kinda sorta maybe avoiding Alex in general. Oh, I saw him every day when we went running, but I had handy excuses for why I was in a rush afterwards. None of them were lies, but it wasn't anything I couldn't put off. I just, hell, I didn't know what I was doing, but I was hurt Alex hadn't told me about his hearing yesterday. The moment I reconsidered that, I snapped back at myself. *It's not like you're giving him many chances to talk.*

Dammit.

"Harper?"

Oh right. Brad was actually waiting for me to respond to his question. "Um, sure."

"Good. Just like before, anything I publish will go to you for review first. At the court hearing yesterday, it was on record that Mr. Schmidt approached you outside of Mr. Gordon's apartment. Were you relieved to hear the judge warned Mr. Schmidt against doing so again?"

My breath hitched and a sense of relief washed over me. Quick on the heels of that was more confusion and hurt that Alex hadn't said a word to me about any of this. I forced myself to stay focused on the question. "Obviously. I'm sure Mr. Schmidt claims it was incidental, but he didn't have to try to speak to me."

Questions were crowding my mind. I wanted to ask Brad so many, but I didn't dare for fear of looking foolish. The hearing had just happened yesterday, but I'd seen Alex this morning... *And you didn't give him a minute to talk.* I cringed inside.

"How do you feel about the plea deal? Mr. Gordon agreed to lesser charges of disorderly conduct. If he completes his community service and stays out of trouble for one year, he will have no record."

"Um, well, if I'm honest, I didn't think he should've been charged, but I do understand why he was. All things considered, the plea deal was fair." I practically had to bite my tongue because I had so many questions, all of them relating to how Alex had responded to any of this.

Brad asked me a few more questions. I didn't know what to think of the fact that he planned to include my response in his story. I supposed I should've known I couldn't get involved with an internationally recognized soccer star and not blip on the radar when he hauled off and punched the guy who raped me. Even then, it was still weird. Brad hung up after assuring me he'd send over a draft later this afternoon.

I should've turned my attention back to work, but I couldn't. It was bothering me that Alex hadn't filled me in on any of this. Bothering me a lot. Even though part of me knew I'd been keeping my distance, another part of me was an angry kind of hurt. Before

I thought about it, I picked up my phone and called him.

He answered on the second ring. "Alex here."

His tone was so perfunctory, either he didn't know it was me, or he didn't care. I was spinning inside. I'd been riding a roller coaster of emotions for too many weeks now. Between the rush of being with Alex, the internal earthquake of encountering Joe, and trying to make sense of how I felt, well, I wasn't my usual self.

I didn't know who my usual self was anymore though. There was *me* before I got raped and *me* after. The *me* after had carefully put myself back together, so carefully, I'd lost touch with who I'd been before. Life was a path of growth and change, which never ended. Yet, when you're forced by brutal circumstances to make changes, you lose sight of what came about and why. In the end, it didn't really matter. I was who I was, whether it was usual or not, I didn't know.

At the moment, I felt as if I was dizzy from spinning in a circle and had suddenly spun loose. Disoriented, I lashed out. "How come you didn't tell me about the plea deal?"

I could hear noise in the background through Alex's phone. Flicking my eyes to the clock on my computer, I dimly registered that he was probably at the stadium since they had a game tonight.

"Harper?" he asked. "Hang on, let me get..."

"I just want to know how come you didn't tell me about the plea deal," I said sharply. From the distant reaches of my mind, I heard a voice telling me to ease up, but I didn't listen. I was angry and out of sorts and feeling like the one man I'd allowed myself to trust couldn't be bothered to let me know what was going on.

The noise in the background faded. "Harper, listen. We haven't really had a chance to talk..." Alex started to say.

"I see you every morning!" I exclaimed, cutting him off.

"Bloody hell, Harper. You don't even give us a chance to talk," Alex countered. His tone was calm, but I could feel his frustration through the phone.

All of it only amped me up more. "Well, maybe you should try harder."

My voice sounded churlish even to my ears, but I was like a boulder rolling down a hill at this point, bouncing into whatever was in front of me.

Alex was quiet for a few beats, and I

could hear his breathing. "Harper, I don't know what's up here." He sighed. "Look, could I stop by tonight after our game? I have to..."

"No, no. Forget it. If you wanted to tell me, you would have. I have to go."

I tapped to end the call and tossed my phone on my desk where it slid off the other side onto the floor. I promptly burst into tears.

Chapter Twenty-One

ALEX

We had a game that night. It was pure luck I didn't hand our team a loss. After the opposing team made one goal, Coach called me over.

"You with us tonight?" he asked, his perceptive gaze scanning my face.

"Absolutely."

He arched a brow. I gave myself a shake. Without a word, he communicated what I knew to be true. My mind was only half here. My heart was tugging it elsewhere. I wanted to see Harper. Now. Yet, I was also a little pissed with her. She'd put up her damn walls and then expected me to magically know when it was okay to try to push past them. Fuck it. Not a damn thing I could do right now unless I wanted to let my team down and leave. I didn't think that was the best choice given that I didn't even know how or when it was best to try to talk to Harper. I'd solve absolutely nothing by letting my frustrations overtake my focus. So, I looked back at Coach and nodded. "Right. I'll do better."

He clapped me on my shoulder and sent me back out. For entirely different reasons, I did what I used to do years back when I was a lad and escaped into football to forget about my father and the cloud of anger he left hovering over all of us when he was home. I sharpened my focus and everything else fell away.

I stood under the steaming shower after the game, relieved we'd pulled out a win. Liam worked his magic and made the plays happen. The final score had been 3 − 1. I dried off and changed. Closing my locker, I turned to find Ethan lounging on the bench across from me. I tended to stay later than the rest of the guys. I loved the stadium when it was quiet and preferred to leave once the commotion was over.

Ethan was usually long gone, but there he sat, his golden hair damp from his shower and his green gaze assessing me. "Good game." He paused meaningfully. "After you got your head out of your arse," he said with a wink. He immediately sobered. "You okay?"

I stepped over the bench running in front of the lockers and sat down facing Ethan. I eyed him for a beat and shrugged. "Aye. Why?"

Ethan leaned his elbows on his knees. "Because I know you, and you look bloody miserable."

I ran a hand through my hair and sighed. I figured Ethan might give me some clarity on the mess I'd made with Harper. He might like to play it casual with women, but he had four sisters and was tight with all of them. I had two, but we'd had such a tense childhood under my father's roof, we'd only started to get close in the last few years. I quickly summarized my call with Harper earlier. It had been brief, but she'd hung up on me and hadn't answered when I tried to call back.

Ethan listened quietly, nodding along the way. "Ah, so you were in a right good mood for the game, eh?"

I rolled my eyes.

He eyed me thoughtfully. "How come you didn't tell her about it anyway? I mean, bloody hell, the whole reason you ended up in that bind was because of her."

"Huh? She didn't have anything to do with it."

Ethan arched a brow. "You don't say? So you'd have hauled off and punched the guy if you weren't half in love with her? Wait, don't even answer. If it weren't for you knowing Harper and what happened, he'd have just been some guy. That's it."

I straightened and rolled my head from side to side, trying to ease the tension bundled in my neck. "Okay, fair enough."

Ethan circled his hand. "So?"

"So what?"

"How come you didn't tell her?"

I glanced to the floor and back up, feeling frustrated with myself for backing into a corner of my own making. "I'm not much of a talker," I finally said.

Liam rounded the corner of the locker row, catching my comment. "You don't say?" he asked with a sly grin as he slid onto the bench beside Ethan. "What's up anyway? You were off tonight."

Ethan glanced sideways at him. "Lady troubles."

I bit back a sigh and rolled my eyes. Before I had a chance to answer Liam, his gaze flicked from Ethan to me and he continued,

"Ah. Well, it's about damn time something rattled you."

I glared at him. "And why's that?"

He sobered. "Just messing. I mean, it's true you're like a rock, while the rest of us have our ups and downs. Hell, you saw me skid sideways and play like rubbish for a bit after my mum died. No judgment here. Is it Harper? Don't know what you could be worrying about. Olivia thinks she's in *looove* with you," he said, dragging the word love out only the way Liam could.

Ethan looked at me and flashed a quick smile. "I was about to say she wouldn't be upset if she didn't care. Take it from my sisters, women don't like it when you don't keep them informed."

Liam nodded sagely and looked between us. "He's right. You not being much of a talker won't help you with Harper. What did you not bother telling her?"

I closed my eyes and dropped my head into my hands. Bloody hell. I wasn't quite so sure how it ended up with me in the locker room getting advice from the two biggest flirts I knew when it came to women. Thing was, Liam still flirted but he was so besotted with Olivia, it was ridiculous. And Ethan, well, he played it casual, but he wasn't the shallow guy he liked to portray.

I looked back over at them and shrugged. "She got upset when I didn't bother to fill her in on the plea deal. I don't... Hell, I didn't know it mattered so much to her. She runs hot and cold, and we haven't had a chance to talk."

Liam twirled his keys in his hand and eyed me. "Maybe not, but that's the kind of thing she'd want to know. So go talk to her now," he said, as if it was that simple.

"She hung up on me."

Liam looked to Ethan and they shrugged simultaneously, their gazes swinging to me again.

"If hanging up on you is all she's got to do to make you slink off, well..." Ethan arched a brow and let his words trail off.

I stood and snagged my jacket off the bench. "Right then. I'll figure it out."

Ethan and Liam stood with me and followed me down the hallway. Once we were outside, Ethan took off quickly with a wave. I stood outside in the cool rain falling. Liam was quiet for a few beats, but I sensed he was lingering. Usually, he was in a hurry to get home to Olivia. After a few moments, he glanced at me. "I told Olivia Harper was it for you. Don't fall on your face over it just because you might actually have to get chatty. 'K, mate?"

I tugged the hood from my jacket up and looked over at him. He knew me perhaps better than I knew myself sometimes. I'd been inclined to think it would be enough if I was there for her, in the ways that mattered. I never had been much for talking things through. I'd still argue showing was better than telling, yet in hindsight I could see the collision of Harper's entirely understandable tendency to be skeptical when it came to trusting any man with my tendency to keep quiet might create a problem. Over something so fucking small—at least to me.

I looked to Liam and nodded. He held my gaze for a few beats and then clapped me on the shoulder. "If I can do it, you can."

At that, he walked away, heading home to where I knew Olivia would be waiting for him. I turned in the direction of my flat. Walking through the falling rain in the darkness with lights glittering on the pavement, I pondered my next move. I was inclined to agree perhaps I could have headed this off by talking to Harper, but I was still bothered by the walls she'd put up. Water splashed on my legs from a passing truck as I crossed a street. The walk to my flat was far enough that on a wet night, it might've been better to take the bus, but I didn't really care.

By the time I got home, I was chilled. I let myself in, thinking I was pleased Callie had finally decided it was worth the risk to come inside. My landlord, who occupied the other flat across from mine in the building, had shown his hand as a softie under his gruff exterior. Once he'd discovered Callie was coming inside, he'd installed a kitty door for her in the back entrance door to my flat. She was now coming and going as she pleased. I worried she'd get hit by a car, but then I reminded myself she'd been living on the streets before. A visit to the vet had led to the vet's guess Callie was roughly a year old.

I closed the front door behind me and flicked on a light as I shook the water off my coat and hung it by the door. Callie glanced up from her favored perch on the windowsill, but she didn't move. She still approached me rarely and with caution, yet she seemed to have decided the life inside was preferred. After the first few days, she was reliably here when I came home. Even though I'd had a shower after the game, the damp chill was enough that I took another.

Afterwards, I stared inside my typically

bare refrigerator. Swinging the refrigerator door shut, I quickly ordered takeout pizza and plunked down on the couch. My eyes kept traveling to my phone as I pondered whether to call Harper. My indecision annoyed me, so I ignored it. My pizza arrived, and I ate in my quiet flat with the news rumbling in the background. I lay in bed later, restless and irritated with my state of restlessness. I missed Harper and yet I hadn't been able to bring myself to call her.

HARPER

I stood by my windows pacing while Stanley paced alongside me, his eyes flicking up to me every so often. Stanley was picking up on my restlessness because I'd texted Alex this morning and told him I couldn't make it for our run. I'd said I didn't feel well, which was completely true. I'd barely slept and was an emotional mess. I was still frustrated he hadn't talked to me about his plea deal, but I was equally as frustrated, if not more so, with myself for not handling any of this calmly.

If there was one thing I'd thought I'd achieved in the aftermath of my life shattering in the span of roughly a half an hour four years ago, I thought it had been calm. Daisy teased me that I was the steady friend, the one she turned to for rational, reasoned advice. I felt anything but rational and reasoned lately. I didn't like realizing that my hard won sense of calm was tied to avoiding anything and anyone that stirred up my emotions. Alex definitely stirred me up inside—in more ways than one. The collision of his presence in my life and my passing encounter with Joe had sent me spinning inside.

I flung myself on the couch, and Stanley climbed up beside me. I glanced over at him and burst out laughing. He was such a tall dog that he looked silly on the couch. His solemn blue gaze met mine, and he whined softly, nudging my shoulder with his nose. I sighed and reached over to pet him. Maybe he was a dog, but he'd been my most steady source of comfort. He offered completely unconditional love and was fiercely protective. I leaned my head into his shoulder. "Stanley, what should I do?" I mumbled into his fur.

Of course, Stanley didn't have anything to say to this, although he leaned into me and let me sob into his fur. After a few minutes, I lifted my head and looked over at him. "So, should I get over myself and call Alex?"

No surprise, but Stanley had nothing to offer to this either. His solemn gaze met mine, and he nudged my shoulder again. He liked Alex and had come to rely on our morning runs together. I guessed he was let down we weren't out today and felt a twinge of remorse. I'd have to sort this out in my own head one way or another. I stood up and stretched. I needed to take Stanley for a walk before I left for work. I snagged my jacket and headed outside with Stanley at my side. I sensed he picked up on my rattled emotional state because he walked a tad closer than usual at my side as we made our way down the street. Once I was outside, I suddenly decided I'd run anyway. I had Stanley with me, and I wasn't going to be afraid to run on my own. I headed to the park with Stanley jogging at my side.

Once we got there, I sensed Stanley kept expecting to see Alex with his ears perked up and his eyes scanning the area in front of us. Much as part of me wanted to see Alex too, I needed to get a handle on myself first. I wasn't sure if I'd fling myself at him or get angry if I saw him. It didn't help that I missed him like crazy and was also annoyed as hell with myself for being so capricious.

Running helped clear my mind as it always had. No matter what happened with Alex, he'd given this back to me simply by virtue of running with me. I'd been able to take walks once I'd gotten Stanley, but the act of running outside was like tripping a breaker inside. A therapist had told me it functioned as a trigger—which was both protective and limiting at once.

My breath came in steady gusts, and I was starting to feel that sense of energy coursing through me when I rounded a corner on the path and looked ahead to see Joe running toward me. My heart stopped and then lunged—a fear-fueled pounding that mingled with my gut churning.

My eyes darted around, and I almost dashed up a nearby path. Stanley moved slightly closer, his fur brushing lightly against my leggings. I started to slow, the sense of fear and dread tightening inside. This was the first time I'd laid eyes on Joe when Alex didn't happen to be nearby. By chance only, Alex's presence had kept me from tumbling headlong into the panic that had once haunted me. Right now, the panic rose inside, fierce and strong. Joe was still some distance away and didn't appear to have noticed me yet. His eyes were on the ground as he ran.

I glanced around and saw a smattering of other people in the park, some walking, some running and a few sitting on benches overlooking the water. A gust of wind came from

Puget Sound, carrying a salty, briny scent with it and spinning my ponytail in a swirl. I kept running, one foot in front of the other, my pace faster than usual. I couldn't say I consciously thought about it, but my feet decided they weren't veering away. I was in full view of enough people that Joe couldn't hurt me. I could and would run past him.

The only noises I heard were the sound of my feet striking the ground, my breath coming in and out, and Stanley's soft padding run beside me. As Joe got closer, I forced my eyes away from looking at him directly, although I tracked his movement in the periphery of my vision. The closer he got, the faster my heart pounded, but I kept running, I kept breathing, and I kept moving. I sensed when Joe realized it was me because his pace slowed. When I passed him by, he came to a stop.

"What the fuck are you doing?" he asked, anger evident in his tone.

I stopped and beat back the panic tightening my throat. I looked over at him and saw nothing other than the cowardly man he was. "I'm running," I replied.

Stanley's soft growl emanated, but he stayed by my side. Joe stared at me and shook his head. "I'd better not have to listen to some bullshit about being near you again." He pointed a finger at me. "You'd best steer clear of me. Got it?"

I stared back at him, anger cracking its whip inside of me. "I'm living my life, Joe. It so happens that means I like to run in the park. I'm not the one who has to worry about what anyone might think about what I'm doing. You are. If anyone needs to steer clear, it's you."

He stared back at me, his face reddening. He clenched his jaw, the muscles visibly tightening. I sensed he expected me to back down, to look away, to do anything other than stand my ground. Although my heart was pounding its adrenaline, fear-fueled beat, and I felt sick, I stood there waiting. Because I wasn't going to keep hiding. Not forever. This was my life and I intended to live it without making accommodations to avoid a man who'd nearly broken me.

At that moment, a woman who I saw often when I ran in the mornings with Alex jogged past us. Her eyes flicked between Joe and me, and she stopped. "Are you okay?" she asked me.

I didn't know if 'okay' was the way to describe how I felt, but it would do. I nodded. "Yeah, thanks."

She glanced to Joe. "Geez, dude, if you're trying to look like an asshole, you've achieved it."

Joe turned his angry gaze to her. "Fuck you both."

At that, he turned away and started running. He cut up a trail into the trees, his form disappearing within seconds. I looked back at the woman who'd stopped. She was, well, she was just ordinary looking. She was of average build and average height with short light brown hair and brown eyes. She met my gaze and shrugged. "Was it just me, or was he giving off major dick vibes? Didn't mean to be weird by stopping and saying something."

My heartbeat was slowing and that cold, panicky feeling was slowly easing. I looked back at her. "Stop anytime. You were right. He's a full-blown asshole."

She threw her head back with a laugh. "Nice to know my instincts were on target."

Stanley nudged her hand because he was ever the opportunist if he decided someone was worth it. She glanced down and stroked his head. "I'm Megan by the way. I've seen you here a few times."

"Nice to meet you. I'm Harper, and that's Stanley."

She grinned. "Aren't you usually here with your boyfriend?"

Her question was perfectly innocent, but my heart gave a hard thump. Was it that obvious? What lay between Alex and me, that is. I didn't really want to go deep right here and now, so I simply nodded. After a few more pets for Stanley, she glanced at her watch. "I should get going."

She was about to take off when I suddenly spoke, startling myself probably as much as her. "Just a heads up since you're here a lot. That guy you just saw?"

At her nod, I continued. "He's not just a jerk. I won't get into the details, but if you ever see him, steer clear. He's not safe to be around if you're alone."

Megan's eyes widened. I wondered if I shouldn't have said anything, but then her gaze cleared and she nodded. "Got it. Thanks for the warning. Now that I pissed him off, it's probably best I know." If she had questions about what I meant, she didn't ask them. She gave a wave and started jogging again.

I watched her form grow smaller as she made her way down the path following along the water. I closed my eyes and gulped in the salty morning air gusting off the water. After another breath, I looked out over Puget Sound. Gulls called and swooped in the air, boats dotted the water as the day began, and the sun's early morning rays peeked through the clouds. I wanted to see Alex.

Chapter Twenty-Three

ALEX

I stepped out of the shower and quickly dried off. After Harper said she couldn't make it for our morning run, I'd hopped on my treadmill. I didn't particularly like running on a treadmill, but I wasn't up for running alone in the park without Harper. It had become a place associated so strongly with her, going there without her only made my heart ache. I'd meant to insist on talking to her this morning and was gnashing against the bite of frustration when she closed that window of opportunity. I'd stopped by her flat anyway, only to get no answer.

A shower after a rote run on the treadmill wasn't exactly invigorating the way a run through the cool morning air with

Harper would've been. At the sound of a knock, I tied my towel around my waist and strode to the door. My brain was half-conked, so I wasn't even wondering who it was as I opened the door. Harper stood there with Stanley at her side. My heart set to hammering in my chest, and the longing I'd come to associate solely with her slammed into me. With her, it wasn't simple physical longing, though I couldn't be anywhere near her without wanting her fiercely. Rather, it was like having my heart held in her hands while my body spun all of its focus to her.

Her glossy brown hair was pulled back in a ponytail with loose locks escaping and framing her face. She looked as if she'd gone for a run with a worn gray t-shirt over fitted black leggings. Her blue eyes were bright and her cheeks pink. I couldn't help it. One look at her and lust lashed me, cracking like a whip inside. I'd like to think I had more control, but when it came to her, I was coming to recognize just how little I had. She looked up at me, her eyes wide, an intensity contained in her gaze.

"Can I come in?" she finally asked.

I hadn't realized I'd been doing nothing other than standing there staring at her.

"Right. Of course," I said reflexively, stepping back.

Stanley had been here enough, he knew where he liked to go. He padded by me after nudging my hand for a greeting and curled up in a little patch of sunshine by the window. Callie eyed him from her perch above on the windowsill, but let him be. I closed the door behind Harper and went to lean my hips against the back of the sofa.

Harper's gaze coasted over me, her eyes darkening. I knew the look in her eyes, it was the look she had when she wasn't trying to keep me out, the look I only saw when we were tangled up and sweaty. My body knew that look quite well. Another crack of the whip inside sent blood shooting straight to my groin. For a split second, I almost shifted to keep it from being blatantly obvious the effect she had on me, but then I didn't. Fuck it. All I was wearing was a towel, so it was near to impossible to hide the fact my cock was hard. I might not be the chattiest bloke around, but I had nothing to hide from her. No matter what happened, I didn't care to pretend like I didn't want her like mad.

Her eyes traveled back up to mine, darkening further. She stood only a few feet away in front of me. She crossed and uncrossed her arms and took a deep breath, letting it out in a sigh. She seemed, well, stirred up. "I went running anyway, and I missed you. I saw Joe," she blurted out.

A bolt of anger hit me. I straightened. "What the fuck?! Did he say anything to you? Dammit, Harper. Why did you go alone? I don't care if you're upset with me, at least don't shut me out like that. He could have…"

She shook her head sharply and closed the distance between us, her hands sliding down my arms to my hands, which were curled into fists. "He can't do anything to me out in the open. It's not too crowded at the park in the morning, but there are always people around. It's fine. I'm fine."

Her tone was soft, but insistent, puncturing the anger clouding my mind. I forced myself to focus on her. Her cheeks had flushed deeper. Having her this damn close wasn't helping me keep a grip. No matter what my mind was doing, my body was focused like a laser on my primal, driving need for Harper. Getting angry was like pouring gas on the fire. I gritted my teeth and latched onto the frayed thread of my control.

"Did he say anything to you?"

She angled her head to the side and nodded. "I think he expected me to go the other way when he realized who I was. I decided not to. Because I'm not going to keep making my life one giant detour around him and what happened. He asked what I was doing there, so I told him I was running." She laughed softly. "I think it pissed him off I didn't just cower. Anyway, even better, you know that woman we see there sometimes?"

"We see more than one woman there. I don't know who you mean."

I managed, just barely, to keep from pounding my fist against, well anything, because I was so fucking furious Joe had been anywhere near Harper. I was trying, I really was, to stay in control here. But I was fighting two competing urges—the urge to storm out of here, find Joe and bash his face in again, and the urge to tear Harper clothes off and bury myself so deeply inside of her, I couldn't tell where she ended and I began.

Harper's lips curled in a small smile at my reply. "You'd know her if you saw her. Anyway, she stopped to check on me and told Joe if he was trying to look like an asshole, he'd achieved it. He told us to fuck off and then left." At this, Harper burst out laughing.

I didn't know how the hell to respond. Still flat out furious at Joe, I stared at Harper, unsure if she was okay or not. Her laugh had a wild edge to it. When she finally caught her breath, she looked over at me, and I realized tears were rolling down her cheeks.

Bloody hell. I had no fucking idea what the right thing to do here was. I stopped thinking and wrapped her in my arms. Damn. There was nothing more right than having her flush against me. I didn't know if I was comforting her or not. I certainly didn't know what she needed. All I knew was I wanted to hold her, so I did. She buried her face in my chest and slipped her arms around my waist. I could feel the pounding of her heart against my skin. I'd like to say I had more control, but my body had a mind of its own when it came to Harper. With her plastered against me, my cock hardened even more, despite my efforts to talk it down.

After a minute, she lifted her head. I glanced down and collided with her gaze. One of her hands mapped its way up my chest, making it even harder for me to make sense of what to do. "I'm sorry I've been..." She paused and worried her bottom lip. Seriously? She needed to stop that post-haste if she expected me to behave in any sensible, gentlemanly manner. "Well, I don't know what I've been, but I think it hasn't been fair to you. You know what I thought at first?"

I shook my head because I had no clue… about so many things when it came to her.

"I thought we could have a fling. I hadn't had sex in years and I figured you were the perfect guy to get that out of the way. Because, well, because even you have to know you're pretty hot. And I trusted you, which isn't something I do very often." She paused, her cheeks flushing. Another dent of her teeth in her plump bottom lip, and I almost kissed her then, but she kept talking. "Daisy tried to tell me that wasn't my thing, but I ignored her. Everything in my head got all tangled up. I figured out I was only okay as long as I didn't care. But I can't not care about you. When I'm with you, everything feels right, so right it scares the shit out of me." That dark look was in her eyes again. "I don't know what I'm trying to say here, just that I'm sorry I tried to push you away, and I missed you. I don't want to keep missing you," she said, a flicker of uncertainty in her gaze.

My heart was pounding so damn hard, it was a miracle I was still managing to breathe. I stared back at her, trying to think of the right thing to say. "You don't need to be sorry and you don't need to be scared. I'm not much for talking and that probably didn't help. I picked up maybe you were after not much more than a few nights with me, but I wanted a lot more, so I ignored it. Maybe I should've..."

She put her finger over my lips. "You don't have to explain anything. Just answer one question, okay?"

At my nod, she took a deep breath. This, of course, pushed her breasts up against me. My cock noticed, oh boy did it notice. I forced my attention to Harper and away from the recollection about what it felt like to sink inside of her. She said she had one question. I could hang on long enough to answer.

"Did you miss me?"

I felt ridiculous because I'd seen her every day, but the days between the sparse nights felt like walking for days through the desert without water.

"Harper, the only time I don't miss you is when you're right beside me."

My words came out rough, almost harsh sounding. But the feeling behind them was so powerful and so true, that's all I had.

A smile flashed across her face. "It's nice to know I'm not alone," she whispered.

Then, she stepped closer and slid that wandering hand of hers down over my cock, the towel between her hand and me feeling rather insubstantial. "We can talk more later, right?" she asked, her voice breathy.

I didn't answer. I crushed my lips to hers and forgot everything else. In a tangle of rough, messy kisses, I managed to get her clothes off, groaning when she was finally bare against me, her skin slightly chilled from being outside. I cupped my hand between her thighs and found her hot, slick and ready. She yanked my towel out of the way, just as I lifted her against me. Her legs curled reflexively around my waist as I straightened and started walking with her held high against me.

With her lips meandering down my neck, her nips and kisses electrifying me, she murmured, "Where are you going?"

"Bed," I choked out when she shifted so her wet pussy slid against my cock with every step I took.

She lifted her head, her eyes colliding with mine. "What for?" she asked, her tongue darting out to lick her lips.

I doubted she meant to make me lose it, but she nearly did. The only thing that kept me from fucking her senseless standing right there was I didn't want to rush.

"Because I'm not stopping until neither one of us can walk."

We tumbled together onto my bed. Her legs never uncurled from around me. A subtle adjustment of my hips, and I sank home inside of her. Because that's what she'd become to me—home.

Chapter Twenty-Four

HARPER

Alex pounded into me—fast and slow, rough and gentle—every stroke sending me higher and higher. Pleasure rolled through me in breakers, the build up to a crashing wave that sent me flying and left me spent and boneless. His body went rigid before he cried out and collapsed against me. With his head tucked into my neck, I could feel his breath gusting against my skin. His weight felt good because it reminded me in every cell of my body that he was there with me.

He started to pull away, and I hooked a foot around his calf and held him tight. "No. Don't get up," I mumbled against his skin.

His low chuckle rumbled through my

body. "Wasn't going anywhere. Just trying not to crush you."

He lifted his head, his warm brown gaze meeting mine. Emotion rocked me and my chest tightened. I had to force myself to keep my eyes open and not shy away. I hadn't really thought much about what I meant to say when I practically bolted to his apartment from the park. I'd only known I needed to see him and needed to somehow set this right. It didn't change the fact I felt vulnerable as hell. Before I closed myself up behind walls and doors, I can't say I'd actually experienced intimacy the way I did with Alex. More like a few comfortable, easy relationships with some chemistry thrown in the mix. With Alex, well the chemistry was so hot, it was like walking through flames, and none of it was easy because he mattered way too much.

I looked back at him and felt a smile tugging at the corners of my mouth. I reached up and sifted my fingers through his rumpled curls. He slid further to my side, just watching me, one corner of his mouth hitching in a grin. After a beat, his smile faded. "You know you don't have to worry, right?"

I wasn't precisely sure where he meant to

go, but I trusted him completely, so I nodded.

He brushed my tangled hair away from my forehead with one hand, propping himself on his elbow. "You worry a lot. At least, I think you do. Of course, I understand why. I wouldn't tell you not to worry because that'd be a bit bossy of me, but I'm just trying to say you needn't worry with me." He paused, his gaze darkening in intensity. "I'm not much for talking, but bloody hell, I got a little lecture from Liam and Ethan about talking to you, so here goes. I didn't realize it was so important to let you know what was happening with the whole court thing. I figured it would be what it was, and I'd carry on. You were a bit standoffish, so I didn't want to be pushy and the like." He swallowed, and my heart squeezed. I could tell this wasn't his most comfortable way of being, the talking, that is. "I should've said something anyway, but I was getting worried myself. You're it for me, and I wasn't so sure where I stood with you. I don't like admitting it, but there you have it. If you hadn't come here today, I'd have chased you down one way or another, but I'm damn glad you're here."

He leaned back, his eyes coasting over my

face. "I suppose I should tell you I love you, eh?"

By this point, hot tears were pressing against my eyes and I thought my heart might explode right out of my chest. I couldn't seem to talk, so I buried my face in his neck, breathing him in until the emotion rocking me had eased. "I love you too," I mumbled against his skin.

I felt the rumble of his low chuckle again. "Well, good to know then. I didn't expect..."

I whipped my head up. "I know you didn't expect me to say it, but it doesn't change the fact I feel it."

That dark chocolate gaze of his held mine. For a beat, everything else fell away and it was just us and the shimmering intimacy I felt with him. He trailed his fingers through my hair and down my cheek. "Okay then," he said gruffly.

Stanley chose that moment to meander into the bedroom and let out a gruff whine. Alex glanced over at him, arching a brow.

"Oh, he must be thirsty," I said, shimmying out from under Alex.

He rolled away as I stood. I glanced back at him and a little zing hit me right in my core. Sweet hell. The man was dangerous. He laid there, his skin damp, his hair rumpled and every inch of his muscled body on display. I'd happily climb back on top of him and spend the rest of the day tangled up against him.

Stanley whined again, snapping me back to reality. I glanced around, realizing I was completely naked and had no desire to put on my sweat-dampened running clothes. As if he could read my mind, Alex stood and snagged a t-shirt from his dresser, tossing it my way as he tugged on a pair of sweatpants. His t-shirt hung halfway down my thighs, but it did the trick. I loved being wrapped in his scent too. I made my way into the kitchen to find he'd already filled a giant plastic bowl with water for Stanley who was lapping it up.

He grinned when I looked over at him. "Stanley drank Callie's water too. I doubt she'll appreciate that."

He strolled past me to cart Callie's small bowl beneath her window perch to the sink to refill it. Heat rolled through me again. Dear God. He shouldn't be allowed to walk around without a shirt. His sweatpants hung low on his hips, revealing every inch of his muscled abs. Even his back was sexy, his muscles flexing as he walked back to return Callie's bowl. I slipped into one of the kitchen chairs while he made coffee.

The morning passed in a lazy, warm blur while we enjoyed coffee together, and Alex surprised me with his cooking skills. He whipped up two omelets for us. I completely forgot it was a workday until my phone buzzed from where it was on the floor with my clothes.

EPILOGUE

Alex

The distant hum of the crowd barely penetrated my focus as I leapt and swatted the
blur of black and white flying into the corner
of the net. My deflection landed the ball near
Ethan's feet where he was in the thick of the
opposing team. His reflexes lightning quick,
he expertly nicked it out of reach from another player and passed it to Liam who set
off a series of passes that ended with the ball
in the goal on the far end of the pitch. Our
offense was crazy-good at moving fast on the
heels of a block on our end. Liam enjoyed
capitalizing on changing the momentum
rapidly. The ref's whistle blew minutes later.
Another game, another win.

I snagged the towel tossed my way as I

approached the bench and wiped my face with it before guzzling a bottle of water. The cacophony of the crowd became louder, although I knew the noise level hadn't actually changed. Not much punctured my attention when we were in play. Precisely the reason I'd fallen in love with the game so many years ago. I was beyond lucky to be good enough to play professionally, but the initial draw had been the escape it offered from my life.

The difference for me now was the minute I finished playing, my mind spun ahead to when I'd see Harper. Home was Harper—heart, body and soul. There were a few minutes of the usual cheers amongst us before Liam was dragged aside with Coach for an impromptu interview. Here and there I had to do the same, although the local sports press here had seemed to figure out I was far less entertaining than Liam and a few other players.

The attention I'd brought upon myself by getting tangled up with Joe had faded. As of yesterday, my full year since the agreed upon plea deal had passed. I'd done my community service at a few different places and at the urging of Zoe, I'd even spent a chunk of that time at a local youth program for lads who'd scuffled with the law. I found out after the fact when I wondered aloud about it to Liam that he'd told Coach about it. Leave it to my chatty best mate. I'd actually enjoyed it and agreed to keep up with a few volunteer hours monthly.

All in all, it was bloody awesome to know I was done worrying about walking the straight and narrow. I'd never worried about staying out of trouble before, but all the way up until a few months ago, I'd worried about crossing paths with Joe. It had never happened and then I found out from Olivia he'd moved. Apparently, she'd taken it upon herself to track him down. According to her, he hid his tracks well online, but she'd discovered he'd moved out of state. That was the best thing for Harper, so I didn't give a damn if he'd done it for his own self-preservation. The attention he'd drawn to himself hadn't exactly helped him. He'd lost his job after a few more pieces in the news on raising awareness about sexual assault on college campuses. He might not have the criminal record to fit the crime he'd committed, but at least he'd paid somewhat of a price.

As for Harper...she was great. I still wasn't sure what it was about that last time she saw Joe in the park, but the brief encounter seemed to have helped her kick off the last of the chains she'd been trailing behind her because of that. I loved that woman so damn much, I was half-crazy if I got worried about her, so it was bloody great to know she was doing so well. Oh, we weren't perfect. Far from it. The first few months after she decided she'd stop treating me like fling material had a few bumps.

I had a stubborn streak and discovered hers rivaled mine. Stanley and Callie had circled each other for months until they finally got sick of us bouncing between our two flats. Callie eventually started sleeping curled up against Stanley's chest and paced like a mad cat if he wasn't there. I cajoled Harper into moving into my place, if only because I already had a kitty door for Callie. We were planning to find a bigger place though. Harper wanted Stanley to have space to run outside. Ever since Liam and Olivia moved into a house in one of Seattle's lovely neighborhoods with flowers and ferns everywhere, Harper had been dragging me all over looking at houses. Honestly, all I wanted was to be with her, so it didn't really bother me a whit where we lived.

I headed toward the locker room and encountered Harper and Olivia coming out of Coach's office with Bentley. Bentley was

Olivia and Liam's little brown dog. He had special privileges to wait in Coach's office. Stanley had been declared too big, although I doubted he'd care to come to our games.

Harper looked my way, her blue gaze locking with mine. I'd gotten used to it, but bloody hell. All she had to do was look at me, and it was like a bolt of lightning hit me smack in the chest. I ignored everything around me and shifted to a jog, catching her in my arms. She buried her face in my neck, dropping a few kisses there before lifting her head.

Her eyes were sparkling, and her smile was wide. "You won!"

I chuckled and held her high against me. "That we did."

She wiggled against me, but I held tight. "Were you going somewhere?" I murmured.

Damn it felt good to hold her. She was strong and soft at once. Of course, my body, as usual, forgot I was drained from a tough match, every fiber attuning to her. Her cheeks flushed pink. "Um, no. But there's people everywhere, and..." I didn't doubt she could feel how hard I was. Maybe I should've cared, but I didn't.

I shrugged and caught her lips in a kiss. Ethan's voice came from behind. "Bloody hell, Alex. Did you forget there's cameras behind us?"

Did I mention I forgot everything when it came to Harper? I truly did. The only press that had gotten any traction about me related to Harper. First, it was my scuffle with Joe. Then, it was that someone had finally stolen my heart. In the one and only interview I'd agreed to answer questions related to Harper, I'd told them she hadn't stolen a thing. I'd had to win her heart.

I held her fast against me and threaded a hand into the silky fall of her hair. I allowed myself just one kiss and then eased her down, tucking her against my side as we walked down the hall.

Harper

My feet struck the pavement underneath in a rapid, even rhythm. My breath came in steady gusts, and I gloried in the subtle euphoria coursing through me. I loved running outside just when dawn was breaking, and I'd had the gift of it back for over a year now. Alex ran at my side. We rarely spoke when we ran. We'd gone from months of easy jogs to using our morning runs for training. As an elite pro soccer player, he stayed in peak condition, so these times with me were just more of the same. For me though, I was training for my first marathon since college, and I couldn't wait.

Stanley flanked me on the other side, easily keeping pace with us. As we rounded the corner on the path where the trees thinned and a view of Puget Sound opened up, we slowed to a walk. I caught Alex's hand and stopped. The air was misty and damp with the sun's rays barely breaking through the clouds here and there. Alex looked down at me, his strong features stark in light of dawn. He arched a brow.

I reeled him closer and reached up, tracing along his jawline.

"What?" he asked, a slight smile curling the corners of his mouth.

His smiles were like little presents—rare enough I loved every one.

"Nothing. Just...this."

I curled my hand around his nape and tugged him down just far enough to kiss him. He dipped to me easily. The moment my lips dusted against his, he took over. What I'd meant to be a little kiss turned hot and heavy in a flash with his tongue tangling against mine. By the time he lifted his head, I was on fire inside and out. Breathless, I glanced up to find him grinning.

I swatted him on the chest. "You just like showing me up. Race home?"

I didn't give him a chance to answer and dashed off. I didn't get far before I heard the sound of his feet pounding the ground behind me. In a flash, he caught me from behind and swung me into his arms. All I could do was laugh.

———

Thank you for reading Big Win - I hope you loved Alex and Harper's story!

For more steamy, sports romance, Ethan & Zoe's story is up next in Out Of Bounds. Ethan is a flirt extraordinaire, and Zoe tests him to the limit. "The interplay between the two is sassy, sexy and hilarious, their chemistry is off the charts, and their tenderness and vulnerability is endearing." Don't miss Ethan's story!

Keep reading for a sneak peek!

Be sure to sign up for my newsletter for the latest news, teasers & more! Click here to sign up: http://jhcroixauthor.com/subscribe/

Ethan

A fist glanced off the side of my chin, and I reflexively swung back. I shan't say I meant to clock the guy right on the nose, but then I'd walked right into this fight. Literally. Blood streaked down the guy's chin while he kept swinging, swearing a mile a minute while he was at it. I managed to dodge another fist and slip out of the midst of the scuffle. It was in the wee hours of the morning, and I'd meant to just skip out of the bar where I'd gone with a few mates from my football team. I hadn't been paying much attention and, truth be told, was a tad sloshed from a few too many beers. I wasn't prone to drink too much as a rule, which meant when I did, I tended to get fuzzy fast. Hence, I'd been making my way outside and didn't even notice these guys in the middle of a heated argument.

A quick scan around, and I deduced I'd slipped my way clear. Last thing I wanted was Coach to find out I'd stumbled into a fight, so I headed outside into the rainy Seattle darkness. I tugged the hood to my jacket up and turned to walk to my flat when I heard my name. "Ethan Walsh?"

I turned back to see a police officer standing beside one of the bartenders. Bloody hell. I nodded politely. "Yes, sir."

I might have just accidentally punched someone, but I had manners. Fat lot of good they did me. Before I knew it, I'd been bundled into the officer's car and watched while another officer stuffed the two guys whose fight it had actually been into another car. The officer who seemed to be in charge of me was friendly enough.

"Mr. Walsh, as far as I understand, you just happened to be in the wrong place at the wrong time. Problem is, the guy you hit is pretty upset about the whole thing and plenty drunk. We'll get to the station and sort this out. There were plenty of witnesses who report you walked right through and took one on the jaw first."

The officer jabbered on a bit, while I put my face in my hands and sighed. Great, this was just great. I don't know how long it was until we arrived at the station, but I immediately declared I needed to talk to someone. I made quick call to Tristan, my flat mate and the mate who had enough sense not to be out at the bar tonight. He chuckled and assured me he'd call Coach and get someone from the team sent my way.

I was a player for the Seattle Stars, a US football team spending big bucks to sign footballers from all over the world. Correction: soccer team. There were many bits I'd come to love about America, but their silly idea to call another sport—an inferior one if you don't mind me saying—football was a constant irritation. The rest of the whole wide world of sports called football *football*, but in the US it was soccer, or no one knew what you meant. Anyway, hard to believe it but I was an elite player and had lucked into this team after a successful run at the World Cup back in Britain. Downside to all this meant it wouldn't be too great for me to make a ruckus for my team. Our Coach, whom I respected, I truly did, had little tolerance for players getting into silly messes.

I leaned my chin in my hand and waited. They'd deposited me in a room that didn't have much of anything in it, other than a table and a phone. I don't know how long I waited, but out of the dead silence in the room came a sharp knock. Before I managed to fully stand, the door swung open. I glanced up to see Zoe Lawson standing in the doorway and almost knocked my chair over.

Zoe stepped into the room, closed the door behind her and walked briskly to the table, sitting down and eyeing me. "Hello Ethan," she said.

I sat down and bit back the sigh that wanted to escape. Zoe Lawson was a criminal defense attorney. I'd met her a bit ago when she helped Alex Gordon with his assault charges after he hauled off and punched the asshole who'd raped his girlfriend a few years prior. Alex was one of my mates from Britain and the goalkeeper for the Stars. Alex, being Alex, had assault charges for a hella good reason. Me, well, I didn't even know if I was charged with anything yet, but all I'd done was basically walk into someone's fist and react.

Now, here was Zoe. Zoe was, well, she

was flat beautiful. I don't know if she was the most beautiful woman ever, but she was to me. She was also slightly terrifying. She stood close to six feet tall with legs that went on forever. Although she must've rolled out of bed to come meet with me, she looked tidy and professional in a navy jacket over a fitted skirt that fell to her knees. Her auburn hair was pulled back into a sleek knot, not a single tendril escaping. I looked across the table and felt caught between impulses. On the one hand, I wanted to walk around the table between us and untie her hair. I'd fantasized a few times about what that gorgeous hair might look like loose, but all I could do was imagine. The unflattering fluorescent lights couldn't even dim its brightness, streaks of gold winked out amidst the rich auburn.

On the other hand, I felt a bit foolish. The hands of the simple black and white clock on the wall above the door told me it was approaching one-thirty in the morning now. I didn't have a good explanation for why I'd ended up in this little mess, but here I was, wondering how to explain myself to Zoe.

Bloody hell. Zoe Lawson had the strangest effect on me. She commanded any room she stepped into. She exuded brilliance and confidence and wasn't the slightest bit intimidated. I wanted her like mad.

I didn't realize I was just sitting there like a dolt until Zoe drummed her fingers on the desk. "Can you handle a simple hello?" she asked, a tad sharply.

Oh, that did it. I straightened and eyed her. "Hello Zoe. What brings you here this evening?" I asked, leaning heavy on the haughty in my tone.

Zoe arched a brow and leaned back in her chair. "It's morning Ethan, and you apparently managed to get yourself in a little fix. Coach Hoffman called me and asked me to come meet with you." She paused and glanced pointedly at her watch. "At 1:30am." Her gorgeous eyes lifted to mine again. They were hazel, layers of green and nutmeg swirled together with flecks of gold.

I got lost in them, so lost she had to clear her throat to snap me back to attention. "Aye, I suppose it's a bit late, or early, depending on how you look at it," I finally managed.

She inclined her head slightly and pulled a small notebook out of her purse. "Tell me what happened."

I quickly summarized and couldn't help but grin when her lips twitched. I wasn't grinning because any of it was funny. Actually, it was. However, it'd be much more amusing when I knew I wasn't facing any trouble. I was grinning because I loved ruffling her. It wasn't easy though. I had to credit her there. But the corner of her mouth curled up, just the slightest bit, and I loved it. Blood shot straight to my groin.

Pay attention, mate. Not the time to get all randy.

"Ethan, tell it to me straight. Did you really walk right into the middle of a fight? Because, I'll be honest, it sounds a bit ridiculous."

I eyed her, knowing it sounded bloody ridiculous, but it was the truth.

Zoe

Ethan Walsh looked over at me with a half-grin and a shrug. Even a half-grin from him was devastating. Insouciance was the word that came to mind whenever I encountered Ethan. He carried himself with a teasing, devil-may-care manner. Pairing that with his tousled golden locks, flashing green eyes and body made for sin made him downright dangerous. Layer on his British accent, and it added up to way too much charm and temp-tation. He ruffled me in more ways than I liked to consider. I'd only met him a few times and always in situations where the last thing on my mind should be anything to do with sex. Case in point, now. It was the middle of the night. I was tired and cranky... and on fire inside. All he had to do was look at me, and it was a direct shot of lust straight in my veins. This annoyed me to no end. I didn't have time for men, much less an in-ternational sports star who was well known for being a relentless flirt. Hell, his nickname in the press was *Golden Boy Brit*.

My wandering eyes—naughty, willful eyes —took in his muscled shoulders and chest. Dear God, even his hands were sexy—strong and just battered enough you knew he could work magic with them. I heard a low chuckle from him and whipped my eyes up, feeling my cheeks heat. Dammit! I didn't need a sexy soccer star thinking I was ogling him.

"Should I repeat my question?" I asked, internally cringing at my bitchy tone. My de-fault mode tended to be bitchy, especially when it came to men.

Ethan ran a hand through his rumpled hair, tossing a sheepish grin my way. "No you shan't. I know it sounds ridiculous, but it's what happened. I was walking out and wasn't paying attention."

"So you walked into the guy's fist?"

Ethan threw another sheepish grin my way, a dimple appearing in one cheek. Sweet hell. He had a dimple that I'd never even noticed. It only added to his roguish charm, which he already had in spades. My pulse was buzzing and heat slid through my veins. Even worse, I could feel the moisture at the apex of my thighs. This was a problem. I was contracted by the Seattle Stars on an as needed basis. My prior interactions with Ethan had been conveniently brief. If he were actually charged with something over this silly bar fight, I'd have to spend much more time with him. Not good. Not good at all.

I opted to completely ignore my body's reaction to Ethan. It would pass. It would have to. "So we're going with this whole stumbling into a fight then. I haven't had a chance to speak with the police. They sent me straight here when I arrived. When I do talk to them, will they tell me witnesses said otherwise?"

"Absolutely not," Ethan said, straightening in his chair. "I feel a bit foolish, but it's what happened."

His gaze was sober and earnest, his typical insouciance gone. I promptly discovered this was more dangerous than his teasing manner. A man as obscenely handsome and drool-worthy as him didn't need to be nice on top of it all. *What the fuck are you doing? Wipe the drool off your chin and do your damn job. If you do it well enough, you won't have to worry about seeing much of Ethan at all.*

The next voice that tried to pipe up got kicked to the curb. That voice wanted to ask how come I was so damn determined not to even consider the possibility of a man in my life. Given how attractive Ethan was, it wouldn't be bad to enjoy some time between the sheets with him. I almost laughed hysterically. *Don't even go there.*

By sheer force of will, I met his eyes and nodded. I believed him, despite my inclination to give him a hard time. As I looked across the table, I found myself mesmerized by his eyes. They were a rich shade of green. Behind his teasing façade, I sensed there was more to the image he projected. *Didn't we just agree we weren't going there? You can't seriously be thinking Ethan would ever go for a woman like you. Not to mention, the last thing he wants to deal with is an almost-thirty year old virgin.*

He arched a brow, at which point I realized I was staring. I uncrossed my legs, immediately crossing them again. This had the unfortunate effect of drawing my attention to the fact the silk of my underwear was drenched. Great, just great. Ethan Walsh, a man I didn't want to want, had the ability to make me wet whilst sitting in a drab room at the Seattle Police Station.

This was annoying beyond belief. What had he just said? Oh right.

"Okay then. Well if that's the case, we should be able to clear this up easily."

I stood so quickly I knocked my chair over. Ethan was beside me in a flash. He caught the back of the chair in his hand and swung it back in place. Ever the teasing gentleman, he winked when he caught my eyes. He was too close. Even though I'd maybe been in close vicinity with him no more than three or four times, he was always a tad closer than I expected. He exuded strength and masculinity. My pulse bolted—if there was such a thing as a pulse race, mine would win right now. I took a step back and bumped into the table.

Ethan's gaze held mine and then dipped down in a blatant perusal of my body. I should've been furious. If there was one thing I'd worked my tail off for, it was professional recognition. Instead, I was furious with myself for the subtle flush of enjoyment at knowing he noticed anything about me. My skin prickled with heat under his attention—it was as if his eyes were caressing me. When his eyes meandered their way back to mine, my breath caught and my belly clenched, heat unfurling inside my core and radiating outward.

I forgot everything I'd been in the middle of. Hell, I forgot why I was there. Ethan stood just close enough, my brain simply fuzzed out, while my heart beat a wild, staccato rhythm. He lifted a hand, tracing a finger along my jaw and down the side of my neck. It was the hottest fucking thing anyone had ever done. I could feel the subtle roughness to the pad of that lone finger, all of my senses attuned to it. His touch was like a blaze of fire on my skin. I was hot all over and nearly melting inside.

I don't have any idea how much time passed, but his voice snapped me into awareness. "Zoe, luv..."

His pause dragged out just long enough, I feared he could hear the wild pounding of my heart. After a few beats where I could hardly breathe as desire rolled through me in a crashing wave, he finished his sentence.

"I shall have you one way or another."

His tone was a touch too confident for me. Laced with his haughty British accent, I was suddenly furious...and more turned on than I'd ever been in my entire life.

Available now!
Out Of Bounds

Go here to sign up for information on new releases: http://jhcroixauthor.com/subscribe/

6) Like my Facebook page at https://www.
facebook.com/jhcroix

———

Brit Boys Sports Romance
The Play
Big Win
Out Of Bounds
Play Me
Naughty Wish
Swoon Series
This Crazy Love
Wait For Me
Break My Fall
Truly Madly Mine
Into The Fire Series
Burn For Me
Slow Burn
Burn So Bad
Hot Mess
Burn So Good
Sweet Fire
Play With Fire
Melt With You
Burn For You
Crash & Burn
Diamond Creek Alaska Novels
When Love Comes

Follow Love
Love Unbroken
Love Untamed
Tumble Into Love
Christmas Nights

Last Frontier Lodge Novels

Take Me Home
Love at Last
Just This Once
Falling Fast
Stay With Me
When We Fall
Hold Me Close
Crazy For You
Just Us

Catamount Lion Shifters

Protected Mate
Chosen Mate
Fated Mate
Destined Mate
A Catamount Christmas
The Lion Within
Lion Lost & Found

A note about Harper's story

Big Win is a love story above all, but it touches on a topic that has been in the media lately - campus sexual assault. It is estimated that approximately 23.1% of female undergraduate students experience rape or sexual assault (Rape, Abuse & Incest National Network, 2017). In addition, it is estimated that only 20% of these crimes are reported to the authorities (RAINN, 2017). Of reported sexual assaults, 98% of perpetrators will never spend a day in jail (RAINN, 2017).

Harper's experience in feeling like the

legal system let her down is all too common for women in her situation. When I set out to write her story, I didn't know how her emotional journey would play out. Time and again, her strength and resilience carried her through. In all honesty, more than once, I wondered if it was a good idea to write a romance where the heroine had such a traumatic event in her past. My stories tend to be steamy, so I had moments of wondering how to reconcile that with her trauma. However, I truly believe we can all find our own happiness. The scars we bear become part of the fibers that make us stronger. Harper was a passionate, bold woman who reconnected with that part of herself in her story. I loved how much she challenged Alex. I hope you enjoyed her journey as much as I did.

———

If you or anyone you know has experienced rape or sexual assault, there are resources for help.

National Sexual Assault Hotline: http://www.thehotline.org
    1-656-4673 (HOPE)

National Sexual Assault Online Hotline: https://ohl.rainn.org/online/

Confidential online instant messaging and online chat with trained professionals

National Dating Abuse Hotline (for teens and youth): http://www.loveisrespect.org

1-866-331-9474

National Center for Victims of Crime: www.victimsofcrime.org

1-202-467-8700

RAINN (Rape, Abuse & Incest National Network)

https://www.rainn.org

ACKNOWLEDGMENTS

I thank my readers with every book, but let me just say it again. Once more with feeling - thank you from the bottom of my heart! My editor made sure I stayed true to Harper and Alex's story. These two were meant to be - writing their story was an emotional experience. Many thanks to Yoly Cortez from Cormar Covers for her artistic vision and her kindness. To Croix's Crew - what can I say? You cheer me on, and you're my last line of defense to make my books ready for the rest of the world. You all are the best ever!

xoxo

J.H. Croix

ABOUT THE AUTHOR

USA Today Bestselling Author J. H. Croix lives in a small town in the historical farmlands of Maine with her husband and two spoiled dogs. Croix writes contemporary romance with sassy women and alpha men who aren't afraid to show some emotion. Her love for quirky small-towns and the characters that inhabit them shines through in her writing. Take a walk on the wild side of romance with her bestselling novels!

Places you can find me:
jhcroixauthor.com
jhcroix@jhcroix.com